NECROMANCY OF THE
DEMON MAIDEN
A Gothic Tale of Podolia

by

BARAK BASSMAN

TELEMACHUS PRESS

This book is a work of fiction. Names, characters, places and incidents are either the product of the author's imagination or are used fictitiously. Any resemblance to actual persons, living or dead, or to actual events or locales is entirely coincidental.

NECROMANCY OF THE DEMON MAIDEN: A Gothic Tale of Podolia

Cover designed by Telemachus Press, LLC

Cover art:
Copyright © iStockPhoto_182789833_duncan1890

Published by Telemachus Press, LLC
7652 Sawmill Road
Suite 304
Dublin, Ohio 43016
http://www.telemachuspress.com

ISBN: 978-1-948046-73-2 (eBook)
ISBN: 978-1-948046-74-9 (Paperback)
ISBN: 978-1-948046-75-6 (Hardback)

Library of Congress Control Number: 2019907234

FICTION /Folklore

Version 2019.06.10

Table of Contents

NECROMANCY OF THE DEMON MAIDEN

A Gothic Tale of Podolia

I. Among the Ruins

REB NATHAN CARDOZO remembered the castle grounds being so much more grand than they now appeared. As the carriage approached the estate of Count P_____—the young Count, he reminded himself, not the long dead lord he had once known so well—he saw that the gates, formerly so tall and imposing, were rusted and tilting uncomfortably sideways. An obviously drunk peasant waddled up to open the entrance for the esteemed guest, although the horses could have easily knocked over the flimsy, swaying structure.

Past the gates he beheld more ruin; the once perfectly kept garden paths were overrun with brown weeds and the bulging wide saucers of wild yellow and red mushrooms. There, past the old apple orchard, was a pond, but the swans were gone. Still, the charm of the garden had never been the plants or the animals, which were merely the decorative edges framing the splendid pavilions, grottoes, frescoes, and temples of love strewn about the landscape.

While at first Nathan could not find the elegant structures he still recalled so well, eventually his eyes landed on a broken wall lying on the ground, with a faded fresco depicting the Judgment of Paris. Discord's golden apple still shone brightly in her bony, elongated fingers, but the head of one of the goddesses had been chipped away. The sight of the damaged painting sunk among the weeds filled him with a deep sadness.

Once inside the castle itself, he was unnerved by the quiet, as if there were no servants anymore bustling about their chores. And there were signs of neglect wherever he looked: Chairs and tables were missing legs, window panes were streaked with black stains and winding cracks, and the heavy dust in the air tickled and tormented his old lungs until he fell over in a violent coughing fit. After the steward finally appeared and had helped him back up, Nathan went upstairs to his room where he washed and ate a light dairy meal he had packed of bread, cheese, and butter.

It was early in the afternoon. Nathan looked out the window. Through the streaks of grime, he made out, in the distance, a temple of love in the gardens, still standing on its circular base with its thin marble columns intact. Yet the elegant garden temple filled him with dread; this was the place where terrible crimes had been committed and where he had once strayed so far from the path of the righteous.

Tired from the long journey, Nathan drifted off to sleep in the grayish afternoon light that weakly penetrated the room. When the castle steward shook him awake again, the sun was already setting in the sky. The steward explained that His Excellency, Count P_____, wished to greet his guest in the library. Please follow me, the steward instructed. He silently obeyed.

In contrast to the rest of the estate, the library had maintained the splendor he recalled from decades past. On two walls were tightly packed bookshelves reaching to the high ceiling. There were even the Hebrew tomes he had loaned to the old, departed Count, who had once had the ambition, never carried through, to learn the Holy Tongue. He smiled as he recalled how kind the old Count had been to him, an outcast in Podolia's Jewish community. Those were the years of Turkish rule in the province, before its return to the Commonwealth of Poland-Lithuania. But the old Count had not cared much about politics—no, his yearnings had been for things hidden and exalted and forbidden.

Another wall contained an immense bay window with a screen door built into it that opened directly into the castle gardens. The panes here were clear and intact. Indeed, they appeared quite new. The gentle pink of the twilight drifted easily into the room through such fine, well-kept windows.

The wall opposite the windows was hung with portraits of the noble lords and ladies who had reigned in this castle. He spied the old Count and Countess, looking dignified, if perhaps a bit uncomfortable and bored. They had both died so young, he recalled.

You must be Mr. Nathan Cardozo. Please sit down in one of the chairs, be at your ease. Would you like some brandy? Please, take some. It will liven up your old bones.

Nathan turned around to see an expensively dressed, commanding young man walking toward him, offering a tumbler of liquor. This must be the young Count, he thought.

Come sit, I am sure you had a long journey, rest your limbs.

Nathan sat himself down in one of the plush upholstered chairs in the middle of the room and took the brandy. The young Count sat opposite him.

Pan, many thanks for your kind hospitality. I drink to your good health and long life, may the Holy One, Blessed be He, shower you with blessings.

And Nathan drained his cup.

The young Count slouched back in his chair and stared intensely at Nathan, as if he were searching for something buried between the folds and wrinkles in the old man's face. His façade of cheerfulness faded away, and his countenance took on a worried cast. The young Count stood up and walked to the window, sighed, and returned to his chair. A lifetime of appeasing temperamental lords had taught Nathan to hold his tongue at these moments and to wait patiently until he could determine what the *Pan* actually wanted of him.

The young Count finally spoke once more:

Thank you again for making the long journey. I was not sure if you would come—it is so far from your home, and I am not certain on what terms you had left this place all those years ago.

Nathan forced a submissive, yielding smile through the heaps of wrinkles on his face. *Pan*, your grandfather was so generous to me; he saved me and my family from terrible persecution. The memory of the righteous is a blessing. But how can I help your young lordship? Your letter was so vague—a matter of great importance about your grandfather, may he rest in peace, but what this matter may be, you did not say. Please, tell me how can I repay the old *Pan*'s kindness and mercy.

The young Count pulled a packet of papers from his pocket and arranged them delicately on his lap. His face twisted with discomfort and he looked hard again at Nathan, as if something about his elderly Jewish visitor simply did not make sense. He then spoke again:

I only recently inherited this estate. My uncle was the lord before me, but he died childless. He refused to set foot in these grounds, and whenever he drank too much, he could be heard across all Warsaw passionately cursing this place. A haunt for demons, he would yell, let it rot. He collected his income from these lands, but would not spend any money to keep up the castle and the estate. My father also would not travel here.

Nor would they speak of my grandfather, whom you recall with such touching affection. He died so young that I never knew him. As did my grandmother. When I was a boy I longed to know more about them, but everything about their lives was shrouded in silence and shame. When I mentioned their names, faces reddened, tempers flared, and I found myself quickly on the other end of a brutal scolding, deprived of my dessert—and there was no greater calamity for a selfish, greedy boy like I was than losing my dessert.

Still, I could not stop wondering about them. I made up stories about my grandparents—that they had secretly plotted against the Turks and were murdered in their sleep after a servant betrayed them. Or they had escaped from the Turks and fled to the New World where they now lived near an austere monastery high in the Andes Mountains.

So when I inherited this estate from my uncle, I was eager to finally learn what had actually happened to my grandparents. This place was an awful wreck when I arrived—weeds were everywhere, the masonry was broken and crumbling, and much of the house had been stripped bare by thieves. Shabby as it no doubt appears to you, it was far worse when I first came here. But I commenced the necessary repairs and renovations, and I also began to bring back a proper staff for the castle and the grounds—although that too has been difficult, as my grandfather's early death and my uncle's terrors have persuaded all the peasants in the area that this castle is cursed. I am, slowly, importing a new domestic staff from far off—Courland mainly.

I immediately fell in love with this library room. I spared no expense to renovate it, so it could be my one refuge in the creaking ruin.

I also walked through the remains of the gardens. They must have been something extraordinary in your day. It was like traveling through Greece or Italy, broken columns and statues and faded frescoes everywhere I stepped. Yet this is nowhere near Greece or Italy. The gardens had been built to conjure a dream, but I was now walking in that other man's dream and felt like a trespasser. I am not sure what to do about the gardens.

I searched for clues that might reveal what had happened to my grandparents. Carefully inspecting the dusty desk drawers and neglected corners, I collected many pieces of paper that I eventually deduced were my grandfather's jottings. There were copies of letters he had sent and received, and notes he had written to himself—the notes were dated, but they were haphazardly scattered about in the shelves and the drawers. Maybe they were once part of a journal, and these were the pages the thieves had not used for kindling the fireplace. Or maybe my grandfather scribbled his thoughts on whatever scrap of paper was at hand wherever he was and then stashed them away for a later time.

Regardless, I collected this set of papers that, when put together in the proper sequence, began to shed light on my grandfather's fate.

The young Count proudly held up the papers that had been sitting on his lap. They were yellow and brittle, and looked to Nathan as if a strong wind would shatter them to tiny pieces.

I want to read some of these documents to you. Here, a page dated 15 November 1680. *The great work is almost at hand. I have finally prevailed upon N.C. to employ his esoteric knowledge for my desires. Sent Ewa away with the children and their tutors. They cannot be here when the great work is complete. Ewa impedes my ability to seek higher truths.*

Then there is a gap of a few weeks. The next note is dated 27 December 1680. *Life is a beautiful dream. Under the light of divine Selene I dance with the lovely nymphs and sage philosophers in our garden temples. H has lifted me to heights of splendor. N.C. wishes to leave, very nervous. His wife is a shrew. But I must keep them. Other Yids persecute him, use that, he has nowhere to go.*

More about this H on 5 February 1681: *H is my love, my spiritual love. Ewa fills me with disgust. I am Paris Alexandros, son of Priam, prince of lovers.*

Then there is a letter. It is dated 20 March 1681, from the Count P_____ to his wife Ewa, who was then apparently in Krakow. He is responding to a letter from her—I cannot find it anywhere, it must be lost. He writes: *The reports of my alleged ill health are greatly exaggerated, if not outright lies. I am not, as you have been falsely told, emaciated and bedridden. To the contrary, my spirits have never been better. It is still best, in my opinion, that you and the children remain away from the estate for the time being.*

Ewa did not desist. There is another letter, dated two weeks later, very short, again from my grandfather to my grandmother. It says: *I absolutely forbid you to return to the estate. I am healthy, and you should stop heeding malicious rumors. I insist you continue to stay away.*

Nonetheless, I believe Ewa did return to this castle. There is a note, dated 19 April 1681: *E and H loathe each other. E has pulled me down from the summit of Mount Olympus to a greasy peasant woman's hut. E is no Trojan Princess. E is a Gorgon.*

But then something happened. The final note is dated 25 April 1681: *E is dead, all is lost. I am betrayed, my soul is damned. H, N.C., the spirits of the garden all betrayed me.*

I found no documents dated afterwards. I checked the church register in the village—my grandfather died on 26 April 1681. I believe my father and my uncle, both small boys then, had been left behind in Krakow when their mother returned here, so they knew nothing firsthand of these events.

I questioned the serfs about what had happened, but they were no help. The old Count kept to himself, they told me. Except at night he would perform secret rites in his garden. The servants heard these goings-on, but were too scared to watch—they were sure it was devilry, some kind of witches' Sabbath.

I pressed them further. You must know, I insisted, who H and N.C. were. H, they scratched their chins, don't know an H. Until finally I found an old drunken peasant who had worked in the stables here when he was a young man—I am guessing a young man with a filthy mind based on the way he grinned when I asked about H. H, yes I know H, he said. H was Halinka. No man could forget Halinka. Turkish girl, she appeared poof out of nowhere one day. The old *Pan*, he has his fun with her while the *Pani* is away with the children in Krakow. Then the *Pan* and the *Pani* die, and Halinka starts fooling around with the Jew sorcerer whom the *Pan* kept, too. But then Halinka, she vanishes one day just like she came, poof into the air. And the Jew and his family go far away. The other *Zyds* around here did not like him. Thought he was a bad sort—heretic to their faith. Go talk to the tavern keeper, he is one of them. Maybe he knows the Jew's name.

So I approached the tavern keeper. Meyer is his name. Such an obsequious reptile—oh great and wonderful *Pan*, you do me such honor in visiting our tavern, please let me serve you myself, only the best vodka, we will drink many blessings to your health, etc., etc. The wheedling sycophant would have never stopped with his flattery except I told him I had little time but an urgent question. Anything for the merciful and kindly *Pan*, he promised.

I asked him directly: Who was the Jew who stayed with my grandfather in his castle?

He looked at me uncomfortably, even a bit angry. Then he forced his smile again and asked me: Why would the old *Pan* have wanted a Jew in his castle? A Jew must keep kosher, so he cannot share in the *Pan*'s delicacies. And Jews make boring company anyway—Jews cannot play cards well or go hunting or do any of the things that lords enjoy.

I did not believe these denials, so I pressed on: I know from my grandfather's papers he kept a Jew in his castle, whose initials were N.C. He and this Jew performed some kind of secret work together. Who is N.C.? Is there a Jewish family with the surname C?

Good Jews, he replied, do not have names like the Gentiles. Take me—I am Meyer ben Yehezkel. My son, may he enjoy good health and many happy days, is Yaakov ben Meyer. You see? We do not have these surnames like you.

I stared hard at this man, and the glare in my eyes made plain that I was losing patience with his lies. After a pause, he finally began to tell me what I wanted to know:

Except, he said, that there were some Spanish Jews who had taken baptism and adopted Christian names, but then fled to Turkey and became Jews again. We did have a few Jewish families here like that once, when the Turkish Sultan ruled Podolia. The Spanish Jews moved here, some of them, from Constantinople and Salonika and Sarajevo. There was a family … yes … Cardozo. But I don't know any N. Cardozo.

Once I knew that the "C" was "Cardozo," matters became easier. I instructed my most trustworthy Jewish leaseholder to track down this family. He then did whatever he needed to do and a month later told me that he had learned, from elderly relatives, that the Cardozos had been poorly regarded and driven out of the community. There was a whiff of impropriety, but no one exactly remembered what that was about anymore. They had moved to Lithuania.

This was a stroke of luck. On my mother's side, I have many relations in Lithuania, to whom I promptly addressed further inquiries. They interrogated their Jews, and soon enough I found you. I was not certain you would come—maybe the scandal no one can recall still worried you? But I am glad you have returned to this castle. Whatever happened was long ago, and the accounts will be settled in their due course by Our Father in Heaven.

I merely desire to know the truth about the fate of my grandparents. I want to dispel the foolish rumors about this place and rebuild it. So please, dear sir, tell me how my grandparents lived and died.

Reb Nathan had been quiet and impassive throughout the young Count's speech, although his heart secretly pounded at so many reminders of those far off days in the castle with the old Count. Should he tell what had actually come to pass so many years ago, about Halinka and the visitors at night to the gardens? It could be dangerous—Nathan and the old Count had together trampled upon the sacred laws of both their communities, and there had been so many grievous sins. And why slander the dead man's memory?

So Nathan tried to dissuade the young Count: Do these events matter anymore? Your grandparents, may their memory be a blessing, were kind, wise lords. Do you need to know anything else about them?

I must know. I cannot rest until I know what happened.

And my relations in Lithuania can arrange to pull your grandchildren's lease holdings.

Reb Nathan shifted his weight in his chair. But *Pan*, kind, merciful *Pan*, how is depriving my grandchildren of a living going to raise your grandparents from the dead?

The young Count did not respond, but his face narrowed in rage. Worried his host was losing patience, Nathan tried a different tack: How can I be sure that, if I tell you what you wish to know, you will not persecute me and my family? You are not going to enjoy what you will hear. I need assurance that, no matter what you learn, I will be unharmed and I have a guarantee of safe passage home.

The young Count swore on the memory of his ancestors and the Holy Virgin Mother that Reb Nathan was pardoned for any and all crimes that may have been committed on that estate.

Pan, I will not be certain I am safe unless you swear it on your Bible and you write out the pardon in a legal document with your signature and seal.

The young Count promptly did so.

The sun had set by this time and the moonlight shined into the room through the great bay windows facing the gardens. In the soft glow from between the trees, Reb Nathan could see the dim silhouettes of crumbling temples of love and broken, crooked statues. The white light fell upon an immense broken marble head lying on the ground, a satyr with winding goat horns and wild, orgiastic eyes.

Pan, Reb Nathan said, night has come while we have been speaking, but I have not properly filled my belly since I arrived here. There is not much strength left in my rattling old bones. Perhaps you have a nice piece of roast meat to quell my hunger? But it must be kosher meat, of course, from the Jewish butcher. I am forbidden to eat any other meat.

He assumed the young Count would have to send out for the cuts of kosher meat, and sleep would overtake the household before the food would arrive. But the young Count had prepared for this contingency, and he quickly pulled a piece of paper from another one of his pockets and handed it to his guest.

Reb Nathan squinted and strained his eyes in the weak light until he could make out a receipt in Yiddish from a butcher named Shmuel for a long, varied list of delicacies. There was a note averring that the animals had been slaughtered in accordance with the *halakhah* by the community's official *shochet*, a man named Aharon ben Yitzhak Ha-Kohen. Reb Nathan was unsettled by the young Count's determination—he had clearly wanted to give no excuse for his guest to slip away.

Well, he reflected, at least I will stuff my gullet with fine foods at the *Pan*'s table. And so he followed the young Count into the dining room. This room was also not as he remembered it. In the old Count's days, it had been a glorious bright place: sky blue walls punctuated by elongated gilt-framed mirrors and in the middle of the room had been a long pink marble table lit by several chandeliers dropping from the ceiling. He remembered dining there with the old Count. Back then, he had not scrupled to eat forbidden foods—seasoned roast pork stuffed into steaming cabbages and venison meat in rich cream sauces and whatever other delicacies emerged from the kitchen each evening.

But now the sky blue paint had largely peeled away, leaving bare plaster walls covered in streaks of soot. All but one of the chandeliers was gone. And the magnificent marble table had been replaced with a modest wooden one.

Nevertheless, the young Count had found himself an excellent cook. It had been many years since Reb Nathan had eaten such a tasty meal. He must have eaten an entire goose, he thought, and he lost track of the number of glasses of *raki* he downed—what a fine touch by the *Pan*, to serve *raki* in honor of the memory of the castle's glory days under the rule of the Turkish Sultan.

After the meal had been cleared away, the young Count brought Reb Nathan back to the library and asked him to recount what had occurred so many years ago. With a full belly and a head floating merrily from the effects of so much fine drink, he began his tale.

II. The Old Sabbatean's Tale

IT WAS MANY, many years ago, *Pan*, that I knew your grandfather. My family had been Spanish Jews, forced to take baptism to save their lives and property. But like other Spanish Jews, they had escaped to Turkish lands, where the Sultan protected them and allowed them to return to Judaism.

I grew up by the sea in Salonika. It was an old city, full of sighs and whispers of longing for our lost homes back in Spain. There were winding cobblestone streets and alleys, and the smells of freshly baked *borekas* stuffed to the brim with goat cheese. And everywhere there were Jews laboring in their exile, but not Jews like here or in Lithuania. No, these were Jews who spoke Spanish and chanted Hebrew in the poetic, sad Spanish melodies.

When I was ten years old, the Messiah revealed himself to all Israel. His name was Sabbatai Zevi, and he, like us, was a Turkish Jew. The whole community exploded with joy. For weeks, no, for months, we walked on air in anticipation of our imminent redemption. We were sure the Messiah would easily vanquish the Sultan, reestablish David's ancient kingdom, and dispatch magical clouds to ferry us over to our new homes in the Holy Land, where every man would be lord of an orchard that bloomed with no labor. Many of my friends' parents sold their homes and belongings as they expected any day to leave Salonika for the Promised Land.

This hope, this dream, was so beautiful—the end of our long exile was almost at hand, and we would live rich and carefree and blessed in the Messianic Age. But Sabbatai Zevi was betrayed by small-minded Jews envious of his greatness. He was brought before the Sultan and offered a choice: embrace Islam or die. He donned the turban and became the Sultan's ward, with a mission to bring more Jews into the fold of Islam.

And now everything changed. Most of the Jews of Salonika—and especially the rabbis—cursed Sabbatai Zevi and denounced him as a liar and a charlatan. They persecuted and beat the few simple Jews, porters and fishermen and the like, who were foolish enough to continue to praise him. The holy community closed ranks, with our learned and esteemed sages leading the assault against even the slightest, even the most trifling, expression of goodwill for Sabbatai Zevi.

Don't look so bored and impatient, *Pan*. What I am telling you will be important for your grandfather's fate. You will see. All these squabbles among the Jews will matter greatly for your noble house.

Some of us, including my father of blessed memory, saw beneath the deceptive surface of events. My father was a wealthy man, a merchant who dealt in fine woolen goods.

His success permitted him to hire many workers, who eased his burdens and provided him with the leisure to study. And what did my father study? He studied secret, forbidden knowledge, the darkest corners of the *Kabbalah*.

With his knowledge of things that are hidden, he saw the deeper truth of Sabbatai Zevi's conversion to Islam. The Messiah, to redeem the world truly, had to strip the powers of evil of their sparks of holiness. All strength and all life in the universe derives from the sparks of holiness scattered and dispersed by the Holy One, Blessed be He, in the process of the creation of the world. The *kelipot*, the demonic husks, imprison and misuse many such holy sparks for sinful ends. To retrieve the holy sparks trapped in these husks and thereby starve the evil powers of their sustenance, the Messiah must immerse himself directly, and deeply, into their impure, defiled realm. That is why Sabbatai Zevi realized he had no choice but to abandon the Jewish people and their special sanctity. He, the holy Messiah, would dive so deeply into the world of sin that he could gather and raise the holy sparks trapped there and thus truly free us all from the dark spirits that deceive and seduce.

My father shared these teachings with me, his only son, but swore me to secrecy. He knew the forces of wickedness had clouded the vision of the Jews and convinced them that Our Lord the Messiah Sabbatai Zevi was the agent of evil, instead of its mightiest opponent. If we were to speak the truth openly before the right time, we would be seized, beaten, robbed, or worse.

There were other Jews like us in Salonika who grasped the deeper truths unfolding, whom we slowly, cautiously, found. We met at night, in the parts of the city where Muslims lived. Sometimes we left the city, separately and discreetly, and met in an abandoned stone tower on a nearby hill. We would share the results of our research into hidden mystical matters and observe the strange new rites the Messiah had introduced, such as turning certain fast days into feast days and celebrations. So when the other Jews fasted and mourned for the Temple's destruction at the hands of the Romans on the Ninth of Av, we would stuff ourselves with fish seasoned with almonds and honey in celebration of the festive holiday of Sabbatai Zevi's birthday.

However, some of these men—too many of these men—grew arrogant and foolish. They felt they too needed to follow the Messiah into apostasy and so they publicly converted to Islam, although they secretly continued to practice many Jewish rites and stayed apart from other Muslims. They called themselves the Believers, and thought that they too could perform the Messiah's great work of rescuing the holy sparks trapped most deeply in the sinful darkness. My father warned them it was wrong to presume to be as holy as the Messiah—the awful, dangerous task of delving into the world of sin was for the Messiah alone.

These conversions revealed what had been feared and suspected, but not fully known—that Sabbatai Zevi had retained many followers among the Jews of Salonika. The rabbis redoubled their efforts to root out the poison of heresy from their communities. As my father worried that suspicion would fall upon our family—his connections with the Believers were too many to be concealed forever—he sent me, then a young man, far away, loaded with books, money, and merchandise to sell or barter along my journey.

I never saw my father again. I later learned from a Believer traveling through Poland that the rabbis of the city had accused him of being a secret adherent of Sabbatai Zevi and led a mob to burn his shop. My father tried to save the precious manuscripts he had hidden there, which revealed the secret true teachings of Our Lord the Messiah Sabbatai Zevi, and so he perished in the flames. May he be remembered for a blessing—a righteous man, an upright man, a pillar of his generation.

But my wise father had arranged for me to escape to a place where nobody would know of us and our troubles. I settled here, in your grandfather's lands, very close to what was then the border between Turkey and Poland. I dwelled among the local Jews. It was not easy in the beginning because I could not speak their Yiddish, and they did not know my Spanish. But they appreciated—and needed—my ability to intercede with the Turkish authorities, whose language I also knew. In time I learned to speak Yiddish passably well—and Polish, too.

Once I was established in the community, I entered into a partnership with an old Jew, who leased and managed your grandfather's distilleries. With the Holy One's aid and blessing, we thrived and I married my partner's daughter, Shayne. Her name was a cruel joke; it means beautiful in Yiddish, but she was so plain—a small, bony girl with moles on her face. Still, her soul was beautiful and shone out brightly from those kindhearted brown eyes. She was learned for a woman—her father had purchased for her a lavishly engraved copy of the

Tsene-rene, a sort of Jewish Bible for women, written in Yiddish, filled with stories from the holy Torah and commentary from the esteemed sages of blessed memory. This book she swayed over and studied, day and night. She would sometimes ask me questions that were not answered in her text, and I would teach her things that are not considered proper to reveal to women. But I had learned from my father of blessed memory that it was the forces of darkness that manufactured these false differences between men and women—she too burst with holy divine sparks from her eyes. According to his persecutors, one of the greatest sins of Our Lord the Messiah Sabbatai Zevi was that he had permitted women to read from the Torah just like men.

Shayne and I did what young married people do, and soon we had a growing family. At this time—such a happy time—I became friends with the old *Pan*, your grandfather. He was young, even younger than me. He had this great appetite for knowledge. He was always buying books and trying to pry into all of nature's secrets. Once he realized that I was considered a learned man among the Jews, I too became one of his teachers—there was no end to his questions about the teachings of the Torah and our holy sages. He even tried learning Hebrew and Aramaic from me, every now and then.

But even more than knowledge, he loved beautiful things. He was forever decorating this castle with new paintings and carpets and furnishings and chandeliers. His wife Ewa, your grandmother, was the loveliest woman any man in these lands had ever beheld, tall and pale and yellow-haired, like the *Pan*'s paintings of pagan goddesses wandering amidst ancient forests and rivers.

Yet the *Pan*'s greatest passion was his garden. Every time I visited in those days, that garden was a beehive of men laboring: this man was planting or tending some exotic bush, that one was cutting marble for some structure, another one fed the swans in the artificial pond—and yet another man was building a waterfall at the far end of the very same pond.

Sometimes the *Pan* wanted my leasehold fee paid early because he desired to build a new marble grotto or pagan temple in that garden. I would ask him, But *Pan*, what is the rush? The garden is not going anywhere. You can weigh it down with even more marble some other time. And why does Your Lordship sink so much money into a garden? You could buy a new estate—or three—for what that garden is costing you.

The *Pan* would smile and lower his head. A happy, light sigh would waft up from within him. His head would rise again and his eyes would meet mine, but somehow look through and past them. The old Count told me that he did not wish for more estates tethered to the ground. He wanted to escape this drab world and build himself a Garden of Eden. *Nu*, a garden better than Eden: not wild animals and fruit trees, but temples where he could speak to Greek gods. Grottoes where he could hear the nymphs giggle and splash.

You see, your grandfather had grown up in a library. With the Turks occupying Podolia, he had despaired of pursuing a career as a statesman or a soldier. And he was too drawn to the charms of women to enter a cloister. So what was a restless young lord to do? He buried himself in ancient books, and he lived in dreams of pagan heroes and gods and oracles and groves.

But he would not accept that his dream was only a phantom conjured by his heated imagination. No, for him, the dream had to be made into something he could smell and touch and walk through. He wanted to be a god, in his way, making his own world, starting with his own Garden of Delights.

Strange as I found all this to be, I thought of him as a good man. He was kind and generous with me and left the Jews in his lands to go about their business in peace. Truth be told, he was probably too busy building temples to forest nymphs to be bothered to harass his Jews. But there are many different ways that the Holy One, Blessed be He, fashions righteous rulers, may they be blessed and live long and in good health.

So, both for the *Pan* and for me, things went well for a time. I had not abandoned my belief in the special, dark mission of Our Lord the Messiah Sabbatai Zevi, but I carefully cloaked my investigations into such higher truths behind a husk, a shell—a *kelipah*, I suppose—of outward obedience to the rabbis who arrogantly cursed and defamed the holy Messiah, may their memory be blotted out. So I had hoped things would remain, enjoying the pleasures of wealth and honor in the outer world, and enjoying my secret studies of the higher truths in the inner world.

Yet it was not to last. Other Jews from Salonika followed me to Podolia to supply provisions and do other business with the Turkish garrisons. Some of these visitors drank too much vodka at the inns and their moistened lips moved freely. They told of Sabbatai Zevi's so-called wicked followers in Salonika, lurid tales about debauched rites involving naked dancing women and men lying with each other's wives. The Jews here were horrified.

At some point, my father's name was mentioned, leading to suspicions about me. While I was out one day, one of the town's *dayanim*, the rabbinical judges—a rotten little rat of a man, with his smug pride in his ostentatious observances of the outward forms of the law—organized a search of my house.

Thanks to the protection of the Holy One, Blessed be He, the rat did not find the texts that would have exposed me as a follower of the true and persecuted Messiah. But I recalled well my father's harsh fate, and I trembled when I looked upon my small children playing in the courtyard. I told my wife to pack her things so that we could flee in the dead of night. She said I must be mad; some hotheads were suspicious just because of the unlucky coincidence of my name and the Salonika heretic's name being the same. She told me she knew I could not be a sinner and a heretic and everyone else could see that too.

I had never revealed to her the secret of my devotion to Our Lord the Messiah Sabbatai Zevi, and I never would.

I brushed her words of comfort aside. I told her I was leaving, and she could join me and be safe, or risk harm by staying put. Something in the sound of my voice must have scared her because she asked no more questions, but packed and waited for the sun to fall.

When the sky was pitch black, the wagon I had hired from a trusty Pole came to fetch us and brought us here, to this castle, where the steward showed us to our rooms. I had sent an urgent note to the old Count earlier in the day, and he had agreed to shelter us for the time being.

But this is enough for now. I am tired—I am an old man, I wear out easily and I have been speaking too long.

Reb Nathan slowly pulled himself up. The lamp in the room had mostly burned down, and there was only a faint flicker of white moonlight from the garden-facing window. The young Count had been sitting quietly, although tensely, and it took a moment for his muscles to ease and for him to appear to get his bearings again in the present. He then muttered the expected polite courtesies about the need for Nathan to rest, apologies for keeping him up so long, recover your strength, and we will resume tomorrow.

But back in his room sleep evaded Reb Nathan. He stared out the window into the garden. There were shadows in the faint moonlight, outlines of crumbling temples of love and of fungi attacking an old, tottering tree. He shuddered as he recalled the marvelously lit nights in the then-glorious garden when the old *Pan* truly walked with otherworldly beings and lost himself in the whirl of his fantasies. It is a dangerous business, he reflected, to dance in the darkness, surrounded by the malevolent spirits of the night—only the Messiah could be strong enough for such a trial.

III. The Old Necromancer's Tale

DO YOU KNOW her? the young Count asked. He passed a small, elegantly framed portrait to Reb Nathan. The two men had returned to the library room after breakfast.

He explained that he had found the portrait while rummaging through his grandfather's old papers. He had forgotten to show it the previous night, but wanted to know now if Nathan could recall who this woman was. She did not resemble any of his relatives, nor did she look like any Polish or German noble lady he had ever seen.

Nathan carefully placed the portrait upon his lap and looked down at it. He was not pleased with the face staring back at him. She was indeed no Polish or German lady. The woman in the picture was olive-skinned and her reddish-black hair was long, curly, and wantonly loose. Her almond-shaped eyes were black and crowned with long flirtatious lashes, and her head was tilted playfully to the side. She smiled thoughtfully while she reclined on a cushion in a blood red silk night gown, which clung tightly to her body.

I know her, Reb Nathan said. She was not your relative. This is Halinka, your mysterious H. I had hoped your grandfather would have burned this portrait, but who knows, perhaps her image is stronger than flames. It is not a safe thing to gaze upon—those dark eyes bewitched and destroyed your grandfather. You should stay away from them.

Reb Nathan handed the portrait back to the young Count, who put it away in his satchel. The young Count looked down and breathed heavily.

Then he spoke again: I have never been able to fall in love. I have read about falling in love, from the ancients and the moderns, and I have seen other people succumb to it. But for me there has never been a flicker of this exalted feeling. Sometimes I have felt lust and indulged, but once finished I felt soaked in my own shame. Or I have admired women from afar for their qualities—that one is intelligent and gives excellent advice, that one can sing beautifully, this other one has a lovely neck and an eye for a dress that will flatter her. But there is no passion in me. Yet this portrait stirred me somehow—I feel I could love her.

Let's speak of other things. I suppose, in time, I will marry a woman whose estates and holdings are sufficient, and we will make heirs.

Tell me more of what happened to my grandfather. He had granted you asylum from your own people persecuting you as a heretic. Is this when you started your great work with him? And when you met the woman in the portrait? What was the great work?

Reb Nathan leaned back in his chair. How do these lords find such soft chairs, he wondered—and closed his eyes. He saw again in his mind the old castle steward receiving him in the courtyard that night, his wife and children so confused with their bloodshot sleepless eyes, but he himself had such a feeling of relief and safety. He opened his eyes again and resumed his tale:

Pan, yes, your grandfather, he saved my family from the small-minded wicked men who would have persecuted us without mercy. I had told my children that urgent business with the *Pan* compelled us to make this sudden visit. They were happy to run around the huge building with the servants' children. Shayne mended clothes and read her Yiddish Bible. I mulled over where we could escape to and be safe. Perhaps to Holland? Or Hamburg? But everywhere, we, the loyal followers of Our Lord the Messiah Sabbtai Zevi, faced unjust, cruel oppression.

In the beginning of my stay in this castle, your grandfather spent his days with me pouring over his accounts. He wanted my suggestions for increasing his income from his estates. The steward and the *Pani*, your grandmother, often joined us.

But then something unexpected happened: The steward woke me violently in my bed early in the morning—the sun had just barely begun to rise—and dragged me in my nightclothes to this library room, where there were so many brightly burning candles that it pained my drowsy eyes. Your grandfather was there, his body was shaking and his clothes were crumpled and splattered with drops of brandy. Books were tossed about everywhere on the floor, opened to pages in the middle.

He asked me to sit down ... here, actually, where I am right now. He paced about silently. It seemed that he was trying to decide whether to tell me something. Finally, he sat down in a chair next to mine, took my hand, and unburdened his heart.

My dear, loyal Nathan, he began, I need your help. Last night I could bear it no longer. I sent Ewa and the children away, far away, and I hope never to see them again. Every time I try to elevate my soul, to fly into the firmament with the stars, and to forget this world, Ewa assaults me with her petty nonsense—about servants, about repairing buildings, about the need to visit some stupid relation or some stupider friend or to attend some ball at some pompous old matron's manor house—and I fall from the stars, fall hard and fast, and smash my bones against the dry, dusty ground.

When I met Ewa, I had thought she was the answer to my yearnings. I was so frustrated then because I had searched everywhere in vain for an ideal beauty. My father, may his soul rest in peace, had sent me to tour Italy, where I had fallen to my knees in adoration of the magnificence of the landscape and the sky, the paintings, the statues, the frescoes, the ruins of temples and villas built by the Romans at the height of their grandeur. At night, holding a dim candle, I read the beautiful verses of the Roman poets—Vergil, Propertius, Ovid—and I dreamt of my own Cynthia, the perfect, enchanting Italian lady haunting the poet's dreams, the lithe quasi-divine nymph skipping flirtatiously through the *palazzi* and the city squares.

But I could not find my ideal in the ugly world around me. The Italians were so tiresome in their wheedling manners and their greed, and such trivial, pointless lies. How debased is a soul that feels the need to craft elaborate excuses for the charges for letting a cramped room with too many flies?

And there were no Cynthias. With my blood on fire, I sometimes could not stop myself from descending into the brothels. Yet the women there were not lithe river nymphs, no, they were nervous and accommodating, and looked as if they had been yanked from a comfortable squatting position milking a cow, dragged into the city, and plastered with garishly thick make-up. Those painted faces were more like hideous carnival masks than people.

And the next day I would be terrified I had contracted a loathsome disease—every speck of dirt or pimple seemed a telltale pustule ready to burst open and expose my baseness to all eyes. I would frantically summon doctors to examine me, but my luck held, and they always found me to be a picture of unspoiled health and youthful vigor. Still, I was filled with shame at my disgusting desires and how they brought me no real satisfaction.

From Italy I was sent to Warsaw, with the goal of finding a suitable wife. I was introduced to many noble young ladies, who were kind, proper, refined, and sensible. They spoke about exactly what they were expected to speak about, and they held perfectly appropriate opinions supported by the most up to date agreed-upon wisdom. I would grope for every excuse I could muster to avoid these suitable young ladies and return to my apartments to burrow my head into the magical worlds of the books of the ancients.

But then at a ball thrown by some great lord or other, I saw Ewa. She was the most beautiful woman I had ever beheld. She was so tall, taller than all the men there, and walked with an easy confident grace, as if she were condescending to visit us from Mount Olympus. The other men stared at her from the sides of their eyeballs, but did not dare to approach her—she towered too much over trifling humanity. And also, as I learned later, her family was on the brink of bankruptcy. I fell at her knees and begged her to dance. She smiled down at me in this arrogant way and agreed. That arrogant smile on her lovely pale face floating far above me—this was my ideal at last, smug and sure in her superiority over the writhing little men beneath her.

We danced through the night, and then I courted her every day afterward. My family was appalled—her people are bankrupt, they yelled at me. But I persisted, and we were married. She joined me here, and she would walk through these gardens like she was the queen of her own enchanted island, like she was a new Circe. I would kiss her in the twilight under the eaves of a temple of love. I had joined myself to pure, unearthly beauty—to the heavenly ideal.

Until the children came. Once she was pregnant, she swelled and grew ill-tempered. She no longer wished to stroll in the moonlight in the gardens, but never ceased to complain about how uncomfortable she felt—always too hot or too humid, her feet engorged to monstrous dimensions—and how hungry she was. Everything I said angered her somehow, and her indignation at my very being—at all I thought, said, and did—left me desolate at first and livid in the end. From one pregnancy to the next, my passion dimmed until it sputtered out altogether.

And last night I could stand her no longer. It was after dinner and she could not stop talking about the many things she felt we were obligated to do—visit this person, write that person, look into something here or there or somewhere. Her voice was like a knife jabbing into my flesh. I said nothing but stared back at her in ever greater rage. Finally, I summoned the steward and sent her and the children away. She wailed in protest, but I ignored her and now—*mirabile dictu!* She is gone.

The dawn is so lovely without her. I feel freed—so much more air now floods my lungs. My wife can rot far from here.

But this joy in solitude will not last, I know myself only too well. If not Ewa, then who will warm me when I grow lonely, as I surely will? And that is when I recalled that I am sheltering you, dear Nathan, from your own people. While I can only pursue the human women around me—and who knows what silly infatuations will stir in me if I grow too lonely—you can reach for far more. I know you have mastered the sorcerer's dark arts through your study of the *Kabbalah*—that is the real reason your people must be persecuting you. So with such a great *magus* here to serve me, for what should I wish?

Here, *Pan*, I recall your grandfather paused. He was breathing fast and his face was flushed. I don't think he knew what he wanted before he had started speaking to me. Then his eyes grew distant—his soul had drifted away, somewhere far away from the castle. I was hoping that he would retire to bed at last, and recover his reason—what kind of a madman sends his wife away for nudging and nagging him? That is what husbands and wives do—they nudge and they nag one another.

But your grandfather's reason was far gone. For when he finally turned back to me with a wide grin, as if he had just made the most extraordinary discovery, he commanded me to summon for him, from the dead, Queen Helen of Troy. No other woman would do—no more half measures, it was history's greatest beauty alone that could satisfy him.

I humbly pointed out that this would not end well. For you see, Helen has been dead for hundreds of years, thousands of years, and her corpse, wherever it may linger in the bowels of the earth, has decomposed to dusty bits of broken bone. I could try to summon the bones to the castle and to compel Helen's soul to reenter them. But you would have no beautiful queen—instead you would have a quite terrified and confused pile of bones hopping about and trying to depart this lowly world and return to the world to come.

The old *Pan* did not want to hear this truth. He grabbed me by the collar and threw me across the floor. He grabbed a stick from a table and beat me. When he had struck enough blows to calm himself down, he told me I could find a way to satisfy his desires or he could turn me back over to my people for trial for sorcery and heresy. Or maybe he would burn the synagogue down.

So I offered another possibility, although I regretted it as soon as the words had left my mouth. Have pity, have mercy, great *Pan*, I pleaded; there is another way to get what you long for. The demons that haunt the world, Lilith's daughters, they have wandered among humanity since the dawn of time, since before even the Flood. They sat cackling on the ramparts of

Troy. They know how Queen Helen appeared, because they saw her at the height of her glory when she still lived. I could attempt to summon a demon appearing in the guise of Helen. But it will not be Helen. It will be a demon—a dangerous, cunning creature bent on your ruin.

Upon hearing my words, the old *Pan* fell down into an armchair, kicked his feet joyously into the air, and laughed so loudly you would have thought the walls were about to burst. Yes, dear Nathan, do it. A demon is even better than a resurrection. You know—well, you wouldn't know, because you are a Jew—the early Christians, the Holy Fathers of our Holy Church, did not deny the reality of the old gods and goddesses, but said they were demons. Everything in Homer was both true and satanic. Your demon is probably an actual Greek goddess, of the kind I have yearned for throughout my life. By all means summon her! When can we commence this great work?

That is when your grandfather first called this the great work.

I tried again to dissuade him. Respect the wisdom of your holy Christian sages of blessed memory, I pleaded, and accept that nothing good results from seeking out the aid of demons. They will spin beguiling illusions to seduce you into their power and then devour your soul.

But he would not listen. No, instead he repeated my own lessons in Jewish wisdom back at me. Nathan, dear Nathan, he said in this mocking voice, I have no fear of a demon who cuts a striking figure in a silk gown. And did you not teach me that all life, even the darker powers, derives its potency from the divine sparks that God scattered everywhere in Creation? Won't this demon have to possess a spark of holiness if it can live and speak and touch?

I agreed that the demon, in its husk of evil, had trapped and abused some holy spark, held it prisoner. But that did not make the demon any less wicked or dangerous.

Yet the old Count continued his mockery: Nonsense, you silly cowardly Jew! God is good, and what comes from God must be good, too. Commence with the great work.

What could I do? If I refused him, I, and who knows how many others, certainly my wife and children at least, would suffer his terrible wrath, maybe even die. So I agreed to summon a demon in the guise of Helen of Troy. But I said that I needed to consult my books to figure out how exactly to do such a thing. The purpose of my studies had been to understand the Messiah's path and perhaps to find a way to aid him if I could. While I had learned much about demons and their ways, I had not tried before to summon one as a bride.

I spent the next few days and nights in intense study, barely sleeping or eating. The old Count's patience started to wear thin. He accused me first of purposeful delay, then of being a fraud. He threatened my life, my children's lives, every Jew's life. Although I was not certain I had yet discerned the right combination and sequence of holy names to use, I concluded I had to try to satisfy his passion before the old *Pan*'s rage got the better of him.

Your grandfather decided to perform the summoning at night in his garden. So when the moon was high in the sky, we went to an artificial grotto near an artificial pond. There were flowers, I recall, that looked black in the weak light. I closed my eyes, and I engaged in *kavanah*—that is, I focused all my soul's concentration upon this task. From my mouth came forth a torrent of secret, dreadful names of the Holy One, Blessed be He, and His angels.

There was a thunderclap and a lightning flash—brighter, for an instant, than a thousand suns. Then it was quiet for a moment before a splashing sound drew our eyes to the pond. Up from the depths of the water came this creature that was about half the height of a grown man. It had goat's hooves and horns, and scales everywhere except its eyes, which were yellow and catlike. It walked right up to the two of us, looked into our eyes, and then laughed, pointing to the ground where the *Pan* had urinated in his terror.

While I was tempted to send the imp away, I did need some assistance in completing my task, and so I uttered a divine name whose sound would hurt the monster but not banish it completely from our presence. It asked me, in Hebrew, what I wanted and why was I punishing it so harshly. I heaped more abuse upon the wretched thing to show I had no fear of its powers. When it was sufficiently humbled, I demanded to know how to summon a demon, which could assume the shape of Helen of Troy at her most glorious, to be a bride to the noble Polish lord.

The imp replied, with no small amount of pique, that I had not needed to abuse it so much if that was all I had wanted. It had a sister who had been a handmaiden to Queen Helen long ago and had helped her to escape with Paris from Sparta to Troy. The grumpy little demon insisted she could appear exactly as Helen had appeared when she had once walked the Earth. I released the creature to go back to its realm to fetch her for us. It scampered quickly away into the depths of the pond and disappeared.

The *Pan* (who, of course, could not understand the Hebrew I had spoken with the imp) moved as if to depart, but I told him to wait. Your bride is almost here, I said. After a brief delay, there was another thunderclap and a blinding flash of light, followed by a splashing sound. In front of us we now beheld a short, slender woman in a simple white dress and sandals. Her hair smelled of olive oil. You have already seen her—she was the woman, or demon, in the portrait you showed me. Call me Helen, she said. I will call you Halinka, my Halinka, the *Pan* replied.

I could see in his eyes how much he desired her, and I shuddered. It is all illusion, never forget that, I said. Halinka smiled demurely and took the *Pan*'s hand. It is all illusion, my love, she said to him, it is a dream where everything is for your pleasure. And she led him back to the castle. I sighed and despaired. But then I reminded myself, what choice had I had? Let my children be beaten or killed?

So I too returned to my rooms in the castle. I nestled up to my wife, who was snoring loudly. But just then I loved that sound. The heaving and snorting and hacking from her mouth and throat drowned out any other sound and left me with the happy feeling that my sleeping Shayne was the only real thing in the night.

Pan, all this speaking has tired me. I am not so young anymore. May I rest and finish the tale later? The next part may be harder for me to tell and all the harder for you to hear.

The young Count did not respond immediately, although his eyes moved from Reb Nathan to the floor and his chest heaved mournfully. Then he raised his head again and asked: Why do you think my grandfather could not be satisfied with my grandmother? I understand why you felt compelled to act as you did, even though the whole business was disgraceful. But why was he so cruel to his wife?

Reb Nathan shrugged his shoulders. *Pan*, he said, how can I explain such things? He liked dreaming more than waking. You know how dreams are; everything just floats about, you can't touch or control what is around you, but you need not have any worries because it all dissolves once you open your eyes again. Your grandmother, may her memory be for a blessing, piled upon his back so many cares and burdens, the children, the houses and the estates, relatives, neighbors, dragging him away from his dreams. And the longer she stood and scolded him in the harsh morning sunlight, the uglier she grew in his eyes.

Look out over there, through the window, at his gardens. They are not real—the ground does not sprout temples and grottoes and ponds. He overran the soil with his stampeding dreams, clearing away the living grass and the living flowers.

But what nonsense am I talking? See what happens when you let a foolish old man's tongue run loose. Let me lock it away for now, please, *Pan*, before it wears me down even more.

The young Count stood up and paced silently back and forth. Reb Nathan worried that his remarks had offended His

Lordship—perhaps it was not such a good idea to be so disrespectful of the young man's dead?

He walked over to the window, visibly composed himself, and thanked Nathan for being so forthright about such difficult memories. In what sounded to Nathan like words he forced out of his throat with difficulty, the young Count made a point of stating slowly and emphatically that no harm would come to Nathan from telling his tale. He then permitted the old man to retire and rest.

IV. When A Wife Learns Troubling News

AFTER A LONG nap, Reb Nathan slipped out into the gardens. The sun was high in the sky and the heat was strong, but he felt an urge to return again to the place where he had yielded to the old Count's wicked desires. Following the weed-infested gravel paths through row after row of old trees, he eventually came upon a perfectly circular pond. There were no birds or fish in it anymore, just flies buzzing around clumps of dirt floating idly in the stagnant, shallow water. Something slimy and reptilian darted away quickly at the far edge.

Nathan walked along the side of the pond. Down at his feet he saw broken pieces of the large jars that the old Count had formerly placed about the garden grounds to hold cherries or dried apricots. These jars had been painted to resemble ancient Greek pottery—the old lord had a special word for them, but who can remember it anymore, it was all so long ago. They were painted, he recalled, with dull orange backgrounds and solid black figures of centaurs fighting or bearded men hunting game or a woman tending a fire. The crazy old *Pan* had brought in a craftsman from the Peloponnese to make them. And now the stray fragments were half-sunk in the mud. Still, he tried not to step on them, out of a sense of—respect? Kindness?

On the other side of the pond was a white marble landing with winding pink veins. Tracks of dried mud covered much of it now, but in the center still stood one of the garden's temples of love. It had a circular base, with four slender columns stretching up to support a little dome. After stepping inside, Nathan looked up and saw that the underside of the dome remained intact—there was a painting of a mischievously smiling, pudgy boy with golden wings and a golden bow and arrow.

These temples of love were where Nathan had often spoken to his Shayne during slowly lingering afternoons like these. On their first day as the old Count's guests, Shayne had asked why they had been forced to flee in the dead of the previous night—as if they were robbers or murderers! What could possibly have gotten into her Nathan's crazy mind? When could they return to their home?

But we will be persecuted if we go back to our home—it is only a matter of time—the rabbis here, may there be a plague upon their heads, will not permit us to live in peace. We are safe here. We can figure out a way to escape, away to some other place where we are not known.

Nathan recalled well the look of bafflement and frustration in his wife's eyes when he had said these words. She wrung her hands melodramatically about in the air, and her response was indignant: Persecuted? Us? You are a good and pious Jew, which any person with two good eyes can clearly see. Persecuted? Why? Because a few rumor-mongers, envious good-for-nothings with too much whiskey on their breaths, spoke nonsense about you following that charlatan, Sabbatai Zevi? No one will believe such lies. You are a good Jew. Could a Jew like you who studies the words of our holy sages be so stupid and gullible as to believe that ridiculous fraud, may his name be cursed and blotted out?

Shayne's words had wounded him. To hear his own wife speak with such mockery and disdain for the Lord Messiah Sabbatai Zevi, who had sacrificed so much for the salvation of Israel, grieved him terribly. But he knew well enough that he must conceal his true inclinations.

Shayne, he said, you are too trusting of the ability of Jewish householders to parse truth from gossip. My father of blessed memory was murdered in Salonika because an enraged mob of his fellow Jews became convinced he was a heretic. We are safe here, we have plenty of money, we will find a new home. The *Pan* has always been good to us. He will see us through this ordeal and help us on our way when the time is right.

Shayne slumped down to the ground and leaned her back against a marble column. Her fist struck the ground and tears burst from her eyes. She sobbed for some time. Reb Nathan stood over her, but she seemed so distant from him, almost unreal—like the fat angel boy with his bow and arrow in the painting above his head. He thought about comforting her, but he could not bring himself to do it. So he let her vent what rage and sadness she needed to vent.

Once she had calmed down sufficiently to speak again, she renewed her assault: You stupid wretch! Bastard! Because you ran away, everyone will believe the lies are true. Why would you run if the rumors were unfounded? Why wouldn't you stay and prove your innocence? So now what are we to do?

Nathan gazed down into her eyes and shook his head. The deed has been done and it cannot be undone. Trust in the Holy One, Blessed be He, Who, in His bountiful mercy, does not abandon His people Israel, but always finds a way to shield and comfort them.

These words had appeased her—or at least she had stopped arguing with him. It was all so long ago. And by now it had been many years since her soul had departed to the next world.

Reb Nathan remembered another conversation with his Shayne of blessed memory, also in a temple of love in these gardens. That was when she had confided her concerns about a new member of the household, a Turkish servant girl named Halinka. The castle steward had told her that this new servant had simply appeared one morning in the *Pan*'s bedroom after a stormy night. This Halinka was now always with the old Count. He, in turn, had taken to sleeping during the day and wandering the castle grounds at night, trailing after her with terrible longing in his eyes.

Yet Halinka never slept at all, or at least no one had seen her sleep. During the daytime she barked orders at the other servants, demanding that they attend to her as if she herself were the *Pani*. But the staff were terrified to disobey, as their lord spent his every waking moment at her feet, trembling with love.

And her arrogance knew no bounds. Whereas Lady Ewa was kind, if appropriately reserved, Halinka delighted in angering the maids and the cooks by tossing their work onto the floor and then snickering at them for being such lumbering, stupid oafs.

With the men she could be worse. She would often approach close to the men in the castle—the steward, the gardener, even the Christian priest who was trying to find out what had become of the *Pan*—so close that if she had moved just a half step more they would have touched. Her breath floated onto their noses and lips. She would tell the men how handsome they were and how hard they worked. To these men (except the priest, of course) she would say she hoped their wives showed them the love and devotion they merited.

Shayne had not witnessed such filthy scenes herself, may such things never happen to us, but the steward's wife had confided in her. That good woman had complained bitterly to her husband about how Halinka mistreated her and the other maids in the castle, knocking things over and spilling glasses of wine and then berating the staff for their clumsiness in not maintaining a perfectly clean house. Or demanding that a hot bath be run for her immediately. Or sending out constantly for more wine and brandy, and more expensive fabrics from which she demanded ever more dresses—always so tightly fitted—to be made. Couldn't her husband, the steward, do something? Speak with the *Pan* about dismissing this woman, or at least putting her back in her proper place?

And do you know what happened? Shayne said to her husband. The steward struck his wife. He had never hit her before, but now the brute sent her to the floor with one vicious blow. He would not hear a word spoken against Halinka, who was the master's favorite, and he might add, a fine addition to their tawdry household—a wonderful, beautiful lady.

So the steward's wife began to spy on this Halinka. She saw her tempt the men and arouse their lusts by hovering so close to them, as close as she could without their two bodies touching and whispering words of flattery. Her husband quivered so meekly when she was near him—from fear or love, the steward's wife could not tell.

And there was worse. About an hour before midnight, unusual guests would arrive. By that time most everyone was asleep except the *Pan* and Halinka. The two of them would stand by the castle gates to welcome in a procession of golden carriages driven by squat coachmen whose faces appeared to be shriveled and deformed from severe burns. Out of the carriages streamed men and women, youthful and lovely and glowing, so many that the steward's wife could not see how they had all fit into the coaches in the first place. These revelers led the *Pan* into the gardens. The steward's wife had crossed herself and fled to the chapel in the convent nearby, where she fervently prayed for assistance from the Holy Virgin Mother.

Shayne demanded that they leave this sinful place. There was something evil and cursed about Halinka, but that witch was the problem of the *goyim*. They had been too long apart from good, decent Jews. This should show him that life among the *goyim*, even alongside their exalted lords, was filth.

We cannot leave without the *Pan*'s permission, Nathan replied. He can have us seized on the road and our possessions stripped—he could accuse us of theft, and the other lords will believe him. Or he could let loose his rage upon the holy Jewish communities on his lands. Would you want them to suffer because we had angered His Lordship? So we must stay.

Shayne asked him at least to promise he would have nothing to do with Halinka.

How can I swear such a thing? We all live under the same roof. *Nu*, I have spoken to her once or twice. She is not so terrible as you and your gossiping friends make out. The *Pani* and the children had to depart on some business or other, and the *Pan* needed extra help running his household. So he brought in a new servant. Halinka is probably upsetting some of the other servants because she is forcing them to do a proper day's work. And if Halinka soothes the *Pan*'s loneliness, well, then, that is none of our concern. And a happy lord is one who will be inclined to be merciful to his Jews.

At these words Shayne stormed off to find their children.

Reb Nathan had spoken to Halinka the morning after he had conjured her. The old Count was still snoring loudly—he would not stir again until well past noon, that first daytime slumber marking the beginning of his nocturnal turn. Nathan warned her that, if she did harm, he would cast her back into the tar and sulfur pits from which she had come. Or he would strip away her false mask of beauty and make her appear in her true, scaly form. She was there to serve the *Pan*'s lusts and fantasies as His Lordship should require, but that was all.

To Nathan's surprise, the demon was not angry or frightened at his threats. She smiled submissively and brushed part of her hair behind her ear. Dear Reb Nathan, she said, I know you are a good man. You are a pious, learned Jew and a fine husband and father. I know you did not bring me here for evil purposes. Remember that, just like you, I draw my life force from the divine sparks that were scattered and emanated from the Holy One during Creation. You may see me as an evil husk, but tell me, what is stronger—a tiny fragment of the light of the Holy One, Blessed be He, or some lifeless demonic shell?

I want to help you, and to find favor in your eyes. I will lift the heavy burdens from the Count's heart and give him the sweet delights of love. Happy, joyful men are generous, kind men. Let me fill His Lordship with happiness, and there will be no wrath inside him to vent upon you, your family, or any Jew.

I see in your eyes that you do not intend the awful things you said. Those blue-green eyes of yours are so gentle, so loving and so lovely. Your wife is a fortunate woman as she can soothe her sorrows in the light of those eyes.

After that first conversation, Halinka would, from time to time, approach Reb Nathan to reassure him of her continued obedience to his commands. She would nestle close to him—for discretion, he assumed, to keep her words from curious ears—and she would report that she was keeping the *Pan* happy, as she had been summoned to do. She would ask

Nathan if he was pleased with her, and her eyes would look up to him piteous and pleading. Nathan would be touched, and he would reassure her that she was doing what he wished her to do. She would then smile meekly and thank him for his kind words.

And somehow, even though he knew what she was—he was the only one in that castle who truly knew and grasped what she was—that demure smile flooded him with joy. He soon looked forward to speaking with her just so he could coax that smile from her lips and fill his heart with its warmth. While he knew this was absurd, that she was not human, still, he thought, she was right about her capacity to bring happiness into the world.

At the same time, his Shayne became increasingly hateful to him. He could not help comparing her plain, pockmarked face sweating under the weight of her matronly wig to Halinka's effortless beauty, her clear, shining skin and long, flowing reddish-black curls. He told himself this was foolishness—the demon's beauty was a trick, a deception, which he himself had conjured for the *Pan*'s amusement. But still, when he saw Shayne's face, his heart sank in disappointment and he wished he were gazing upon Halinka instead.

It did not help that Shayne's face was now frequently twisted with rage. She could not conceal her hatred of her husband for trapping her and her children in that hideous, *goyische* castle with the lecherous Count and his disgusting mistress, Halinka. At best, she was curt with him, but often she would seek out opportunities, even on slim pretext, to insult and belittle her husband. So if Nathan forgot to send out for the exact type of food that the children wanted or to give them a sufficiently rigorous lesson in a small point of Hebrew grammar (as Shayne did not wish their prolonged absence from *cheder* to turn them into ignorant boors), she would explode with curses and could not be appeased. Nathan would finally be forced to flee from her, usually into one of the garden grottoes. And there he would find himself, to his surprise and disgust, wishing that he could lay his head upon Halinka's lap and unburden his soul to her.

And now, sitting in the ruins of the same gardens, Nathan felt a stabbing pain in his breast as he recalled how he had behaved in those far off days. He had buried his Shayne four years ago, and afterwards he had rebuffed all offers of remarriage. Shayne had been a wise and pious woman. He missed her often now, missed her simply being in a room with him bustling about a stove or a pantry.

Soon the young *Pan* will want to hear more, he thought. Best to leave the gardens and fill my belly inside, make sure I will have the strength to continue telling the tale of the old *Pan* and *Pani*.

So with heavy, slow steps, Reb Nathan returned to the castle.

V. Enchanted Nights in the Pagan Gardens

IT WAS EVENING now in the castle's library, and the moon shone brightly through the large garden window. The young Count had not lit the lamps or brought a candle, so everything Reb Nathan beheld was an outline of shadow and silhouette.

Have dinner and brandy restored your strength, old man? Are you prepared to tell what happened between my grandfather and Halinka?

Although he had readied himself to continue telling the tale, Reb Nathan still felt wary. Why did this young lord want to force him to recall such painful, distant days? But could he stop now that he had traveled back here and started the tale? He should never have returned here—he should have excused himself on grounds of ill health brought on by extreme old age.

But no—he somehow enjoyed dwelling on these events. What had happened afterwards in his life was a quiet, sheepish atonement for his crimes in this castle and a retreat into deliberately, almost ostentatiously, dull living—eat, sleep, defecate, and do it all far away from demons. While comfortable, those dutiful, blameless years had snuffed out the glow that had been so bright when Halinka haughtily strutted through these halls.

Old Jew—the young Count's irritated tone woke him from his musings—are you going to speak again? Let's start somewhere simple: Who painted Halinka's portrait? I cannot stop gazing upon it. She seems alive, feral—I can hear her blood pump and see her lips sweat. What kind of painter can imbue his subject with such power, even long after death?

Reb Nathan looked down at the carpet on the floor. *Pan*, neither subject nor painter are dead. I am not sure they can die. The portrait painter was one of the garden people, the night people—if people is the right word for what they were.

After I had summoned Halinka for your grandfather that night, she lay with him in his bed for the few hours left before dawn. He was so exhausted afterwards that he did not rise again until twilight. And so began his new habits with Halinka: He would rise at dusk, frolic through the night with Halinka, and collapse in sleep just before dawn.

But they did more than merely share a bed as if they were husband and wife. Halinka was a crafty one—she knew he would grow bored with her if there were nothing else to entertain him. So she would take him in the evenings to the castle gate, where she would welcome the visitors. These nighttime guests would arrive in magnificent carriages, grander than any carriages owned by any lords or ladies near this estate. They would burst forth from the carriage doors, troops of men and women, and follow Halinka and the *Pan* into the gardens. The guests were always immaculately dressed, and young, and beautiful.

For several nights I observed their arrival from inside the castle. Finally, I asked His Lordship if I could accompany him the next time they came. After all, these had to be demons—they did not resemble any of the human inhabitants of the region as far as I knew. I warned that he might need my assistance—I alone had the knowledge to tame them if that became necessary.

Yet the old Count refused my offer. They fear you and so does Halinka, he told me. I am concerned your presence would scare them away. They are my friends, my first true friends. I cannot have you upset them with your sorcerer's threats and evil eyes.

But *Pan*, I replied, you cannot believe these are people? Their beauty, their carriages, their clothes, it is all illusion and deception. They will only cause you harm. Let me protect you.

No, he said, I cannot let you do that.

Then *Pan*, I said, please permit me and my family to depart. You have the bride you sought. Let us go far away and leave you in peace.

No, I cannot do that, he said back to me. You know the terrible secret of Halinka's true nature, beneath her enticing surface—you know it better than I ever shall—and I cannot chance that you will reveal it. And I may need your services again someday—who knows, Halinka may become dangerous, or maybe I will want another new bride. So you are to remain here, for the time being, as my honored and esteemed guest.

What did Halinka, her friends, and your grandfather do all night? None of these companions of hers ever entered the castle itself. I sometimes spied on them from the windows in my rooms or the hallways, when I thought they would not notice. There were always bright lights, like a thousand chandeliers were hanging over the garden grounds, but there was no source for this abundant light—no torches, no candles, no fire. It simply appeared when they appeared.

There were the laurel wreaths that they passed around and used to adorn their heads. Sometimes they also donned the clothing of the Greeks and the Romans.

There were barrels of wine that would materialize from nowhere, which they would drink from large orange chalices with black bearded figures painted on them.

Yes, and there was music. Instruments would suddenly emerge from the air and the guests would put on concerts in the artificial grottoes. Your grandfather would dance to this music with abandon—he danced with Halinka, he danced with the other female demons. They passed him around in a drunken smiling haze.

Sometimes the group would stroll through the garden paths. Your grandfather's words seemed to elicit laughter and cheer from his companions, although I could not hear what anyone said.

Then there was the strange business of their food. The old *Pan* now took only one meal in the castle itself—his breakfast at twilight. I never saw them sit down for a meal in the gardens. But every so often Halinka would reach up into the air as if she were picking fruit from a tree, and a long red fruit, shaped like a cucumber would appear. She would feed these to your grandfather, who gobbled them up like a greedy little boy.

And one night—yes, now I recall it—there was a portrait painter. He set up his easel and canvas next to the largest of the artificial ponds. Each guest of the garden party sat for a portrait, including Halinka and your grandfather. I do not know what happened to his portrait, but what you found was Halinka's portrait from that night. It sings to you because it is enchanted. Don't look at it too often. I would tell you to burn it, but I am not sure the flames can be of any help. Try to put it away and keep it out of sight. It will poison your soul.

While your grandfather danced and laughed and ate and drank through the nights, the servants in the castle grew steadily more alarmed. Halinka, who did not sleep, roamed the hallways in the daytime berating them, knocking over their work, and demanding they redo it. Sometimes I was forced to intervene, as I was the only human being whom she feared.

Although the old *Pan* had explained to his staff that Halinka was a new Turkish servant girl whom he had engaged, no one believed him. The rumors swirled, with the consensus that she was some sort of harlot with whom he had fallen madly in love when he had traveled to Italy. My wife was disgusted by her, and she wanted us to keep our distance.

And then His Lordship's health took a turn for the worse. His eyes and cheeks hollowed out, and then his skin wrinkled and folded over. Soon his hair turned white and started falling out. He lost so much weight that his skeletal frame staggered and stumbled about uneasily. When I watched him in the gardens at night he no longer danced, but leaned pitifully on Halinka for support.

I was worried. The *Pan* had always been my protector. And if he should die mysteriously here, with me as his guest, what might suspicious tongues say? So I made up my mind to confront Halinka.

But first I fasted for three days, abstained from lying with my wife, and studied and prayed without stop. I emptied my soul of all the profane matter that weighed it down in this lowly and filthy world, and when I was light as a feather, I drifted off into the upper realms and beheld marvelous visions. I met an angel, a kindly creature, who quenched my thirst with water from the Garden of Eden. The angel told me to do what needed doing at noon on the next day, when the sun would be brightly lit, weakening the strength of night creatures like demons.

And when that time came, I sat down in this room in a chair like these, and uttered a terrible combination of holy and angelic names, concentrating intensely, with my eyes closed, on the image of each Hebrew letter. For you see, Hebrew is not simply another language like French or Polish. It is the language of the Holy One's celestial court. While the Holy One, Blessed be He, of course knows all languages, His angels speak only Hebrew. And so, only Hebrew letters, harnessed by powerful concentration and a purified soul, can fully compel the enchantments of the angelic host.

When I opened my eyes, there was Halinka at my feet, shivering miserably. Her feet and hands had been shackled by the heavenly spirits whom I had summoned to assist me.

Yet at the same time there was a healthy glow all through her. She had always been beautiful in her illusion, her imitation, of Helen of Troy. But that beauty had something decayed about it— as if she had been recovering from a long illness. Now, though, she had such lively color everywhere—her skin, her eyes, her hair. It was as if she had eaten and drunk nothing but the pure light of Creation for weeks on end.

I went right to the point: Foul demon imp, what are you doing to your human bridegroom? He eats and drinks with abandon in the gardens at night, but he wastes away like a starving man.

She grasped my leg with her bound hands and rubbed her head against it, like an affectionate cat. She moaned at me: Oh mighty *ba'al shem*—that is the term we Jews use for a man deeply learned in secret lore, who knows how to wield the power of holy names—please have mercy on me, I am suffering terribly. You forced me to come here, you made me dress my flesh in the costume of this wicked man's sordid fantasies and you gave me as a bride to him. He compels me to entertain him all through the night and insists on taking his pleasure with my body for hours on end. His debauchery is wasting his body away. He does nothing but indulge in the basest, grossest excesses of drink, of touch, of everything.

I warned him—I told him the pleasures I offered were different and more consuming than what a real human woman could give him, that it was an enchantment, so he must only taste a little at a time. But he cannot stop himself from gorging.

I tried to resist him, for his own good. I said to him, Please, I beg you, no more, My Lord, don't make me hurt you so. But he said it was pleasure, greater than any other that he craved, and that if I refused him, he would order you, his pet Jew sorcerer, to torture and flay me until I gave him what he wanted. And so I yielded to him under duress, again and again.

Have I now done something to anger him? Am I being punished? Please, don't make me suffer more.

As she pleaded with me she looked into my eyes with great emotion. At that moment I could not bear for her to be so upset. Even though I knew what she was, I felt a desperate desire to make her suffering end, as if that were the only way I could ease the pounding in my temples and my pulse. So I released Halinka from her bonds with a feeble warning that I could summon spirits to act against her again, and she must make sure no further harm comes to the *Pan*. She stood up next to me, very close but not touching, and took my hands in hers. She tilted her head a little to the side and smiled warmly. I could hardly breathe in my excitement. We shall look after the *Pan*'s good health together, as his dear devoted friends, she said. And then she walked away, in triumph.

For you see, the glow within her skin and her eyes was no reflection of the sunlight. She had grown strong, much stronger, because she had been feeding greedily off the sparks of holiness and divine light she had found within your grandfather—she was eating his soul. And my incantations and mystical lore were not so mighty against her anymore.

On the other hand, my heart would sink at the sight of my wife, with her pestering and haranguing about how I ignored the children and their education, how I was doing nothing to help our family escape this awful castle and live a normal life again among good Jews.

Her words filled me with rage, and I met reproach with reproach. I have kept us alive by keeping the *Pan*'s favor, I thundered at her, and your good Jews want to murder us, just as the good Jews of Salonika murdered my father. My Shayne, may she rest in peace upon a golden throne in Paradise, became ugly, repulsive to me—she looked like a rat, I thought, and smelled like an outhouse.

I slavishly followed Halinka around the castle. After a while, she put me to work doing errands for her. In the beginning, these were small—fetch a glass or bring clothes over to her. But before I realized what had happened, I was giving her baths and brushing her hair and massaging her feet. I helped her to dress for the old Count, like I was her handmaiden. She smirked and laughed at me as I rushed to do her will, but so drunk was my soul on her black almond eyes and blood red lips, I lost all regard for my dignity.

Beware, young *Pan*, your eyes will deceive you. You think they see, but they see only illusions and lies, the deceptions spun by the evil husks that permeate this lowly material world.

Fortunately, there are always some who refuse to be taken in by illusion. The good servants of this castle, especially the maids who had attended upon your grandmother, had grown alarmed and suspicious. They had written to the *Pani*, Lady Ewa, and she returned to the castle—but wisely, without her children.

Upon her arrival, your grandmother consulted the servants and inspected her husband's condition. She was aghast at the sight of him—wrinkles had spread everywhere across his deathly pale skin, all the hair on his body had fallen out, and he was too weak to move about without help. Halinka had rushed in, pretending to be concerned at the old Count's ill health. But when the *Pani* turned to look at the demon, she screamed, grabbed a broom, and beat Halinka viciously until she drove her away. She later told the servants, who later told me, that she had seen snakes writhing about in Halinka's hair and hordes of yellow and black striped wasps, with pointed stingers, buzzing about her waist and chest.

Lady Ewa sat by her husband's bed and tried to nurse him back to health. My wife, my Shayne, helped her, along with the servants. They gave him plentiful helpings of food and drink, but to no avail—he gained not one bit of strength. It was as if the food vanished into the air once it passed his lips.

The old *Pan* could not sleep, and his eyes were always half-open. The room had to be kept nearly pitch dark—light, any bright light at least, made him wail like a wounded dog. He often asked where was Halinka, where were the wonderful people in the gardens.

The *Pani* sent for the doctor. After examining the patient for an hour, the doctor pronounced him in fine health for a man so old and frail. He urged the *Pani*, whom he took for the patient's granddaughter, to help ease the old man's last days. She was too shaken by these words to have the presence of mind to correct the doctor. When your grandmother recovered her senses, she understood that medicine would be of no use.

She now sent for the abbot of the nearby monastery, Brother Medardus. I knew him slightly, from business dealings with his order here and there. When Shayne told me he was coming to the castle, I shuddered in terror. He knew a great deal about demons, certainly more than I did. For you see, in those days Brother Medardus was a famous penitent. He had been renowned in his youth as a spellbinding preacher, but in his pride and arrogance he had been seduced by a demon who posed as a beautiful noblewoman seeking confession. She fed him the sweet blue liqueur that the demons imbibe, until he was drunk with lust and rage. He ran off with her and the pair committed many crimes. But eventually he saw the error of his ways, repented, and lived an exemplary life of prayer, charity, and study.

I feared that Brother Medardus would discern what had happened and grasp my part in it. I considered flight, but that would only make my guilt appear to be certain and, anyway, I could not have brought myself to leave Halinka. Exiled from the *Pan*'s presence by Lady Ewa, she had insisted I stay by her side for hours at a time. She demanded ever more demeaning tasks from me—I had to wash her feet and to clean her sheets and to apply her cosmetics and perfumes.

When I learned that Brother Medardus was coming, I warned Halinka that we were both likely to be exposed for our crimes—he was too wise, too pious, to be deceived by her demon's ruses. But she told me not to worry. She was entirely confident, she said, that the monk would take pity upon her and realize that the old Count had brought his illness down upon himself. The monk was a good man, and she trusted in his compassion.

Brother Medardus examined your grandfather and pronounced this to be a case of witchcraft, because there was no natural cause for a man's physical life span slipping away so rapidly. He asked the old Count how had this happened? If you have sins to confess, do so now and repent. You have lost this world, but you can still gain eternal life and salvation.

The *Pan* moaned about how he loved Halinka, how she was his true bride, how she possessed a beauty and a charm that were more than human. The monk asked: Have you had adulterous relations with this Halinka? But your grandfather, still delirious, said it was not adultery because he had the right to lie with his true bride.

Brother Medardus pressed on: Where did she come from, this Halinka? When did she arrive at this castle?

The old Count told the truth, in his half-mad way. He said: We summoned her and she emerged from the water, like Aphrodite. But not Aphrodite. Helen of Troy, daughter of mighty Zeus and Queen Leda of Sparta.

The monk asked: And from what water did she emerge?

From a pond in my garden, the old *Pan* replied with a broad smile. She walked up to me and the Jew sorcerer.

At these words, your grandmother ordered that Halinka and I be put in chains and locked in the castle dungeon, a dark and damp place filled with rats and maggots. I was put in one small cell, Halinka in another.

Alone now, I was able to purify my soul of the enchantment of Halinka's glowing black eyes. I wept bitterly in remorse for my horrible sins and begged the Holy One, Blessed be He, to forgive me and to bestow His mercy and kindness upon my wife and children, whom I had led into such danger. Although I had no book with me to study, I cleansed myself through prayer and intense concentration upon words from the holy *Torah* that I had long ago committed to memory.

I grew faint from hunger and thirst—had I been left to die in this cell? If that is to be the price of my penance, I thought, then let it come to pass—I will not doubt His ways, Blessed is the One Righteous and True Judge. I will offer my body as sacrifice and atonement to gain eternal life in the World to Come. I swore that I would intercede before the Throne of Glory in the Heavenly Court on behalf of my wife Shayne and my children.

Shayne! So late did I now finally understand how fortunate I had been to have had such an upright bride. She had not been tricked by Halinka's illusions or by my cowardly lies. Shayne had seen the truth from the beginning, but I had not heeded her wise words.

And as I dragged my weak body to lean against a moldy, rotting wall, ready to await my end in peace, a light filled the cell, like a small sun had been set there just for me. From out of this light appeared *Eliyahu HaNavi*, the Prophet Elijah. He handed me a pitcher of water to drink, so sweet and delicious—it was water from Paradise, from the Garden of Eden itself. That water healed my wounds and restored my strength.

Elijah spoke to me: You are a learned scholar, so I will not hide who I am from you. Your prayers have moved the Heavenly Court to tears, and the Holy One, Blessed be He, has taken pity upon you. I place this amulet around your neck—and he placed around my neck a string holding a square green box. I felt the box and could tell there was a scroll inside—holy names written by an angel's scribal hand.

Elijah continued: This amulet will remove the fog of illusion from your eyes. Now go, do the things that you need to do with your body healed and your true sight restored.

He disappeared. But the light remained, although a bit dimmer; and I saw the cell door open for me. I walked out and went back upstairs—no one had been posted to guard me.

When I arrived upstairs there were servants wailing and running in every direction. What had happened? I asked. But no one heeded me.

I went to my room and found Shayne. I told her how I had been miraculously saved and asked her what had sent the castle into such chaos. She burst into tears and said the *Pani* had departed from this life.

I said: But you must mean the *Pan*, who was so ill? The *Pani* is young, healthy, how could she be the one to die?

But Shayne's only response was more tears.

I knew immediately that Halinka had done something terrible—human chains must have not been strong enough to hold her in the dungeon, and she must have broken free to exact her revenge. I went to Halinka's room, where she lay immodestly on her sheets, in a red robe that only half covered her body. On the floor beside her bed was a golden platter on which sat the *Pani*'s severed head.

Halinka smiled serenely, as if she had never been imprisoned, and asked me to bring her hair brush. But thanks to Elijah's amulet, I now beheld this creature as she truly was: I saw her feet were hooves, her skin was covered with green scales, and her hair was a tangle of snakes. Her eyes had no luster—they looked like glass ovals that had been painted to resemble human eyes.

I pulled out the amulet from beneath my shirt and gripped it tightly. What have you done? I thundered at Halinka. Where is Brother Medardus?

Before she could answer I uttered many powerful combinations of the Hebrew letters of the various true, hidden names of the Holy One, Blessed be He. She shrieked in pain.

I once more demanded she answer me.

But all she did was scream and hiss. So I invoked more holy names, and harnessing their great might, cast Halinka back to the foul realm from which she had originally come.

I looked for the castle steward and told him that Halinka had fled. I directed him to find the pieces of Lady Ewa's body for proper burial.

I was determined to cleanse this place of all corruption. So I went next to the *Pan*'s bedroom, thinking there must be some way I could save him.

He was moaning and weak, a pile of writhing, rattling bones. He had trouble recognizing me at first. He said in a whisper that his eyesight was almost gone, and no matter how hard he tried, he could only see lines and shadows.

I sat down and took his hand in mine. I told the *Pan* I had banished Halinka back to her own kind, but I had been unable to do so before the demon had murdered the *Pani*. I expressed my great sorrow at her unjust death, but assured him that the Heavenly Court would no doubt judge her a righteous and brave woman and seat her upon a golden throne while she waited for her husband to join her.

The *Pan* said to me: I was told that Ewa had died. I am too frail to bear such a loss. It is only too late that I now see my error, my folly, in chasing evil spirits instead of seeking the love of my good Christian wife. I have not much longer to live. Where is Brother Medardus or another priest? I need to confess my sins—I have done terrible things, without the Church's absolution, I am damned for eternity.

The monk was nowhere to be seen, and I worried that a priest might not arrive in time. So to atone for the wrong I had earlier done by giving in to the old Count's wicked whims, I summoned an archangel through the appropriate combination of sacred names and letters and commanded him to bring the spirit of a Christian saint to hear the *Pan*'s confession and to absolve him of his sins.

And in an instant a holy Christian saint appeared—do not ask me which one, your Church has so many, but the *Pan* recognized him and acknowledged his authority—that holy saint, as I was saying, heard your grandfather's confession and then blessed the *Pan* and cleansed him of all sin. With his soul now purified, the saint gently lifted his spirit away from his body, and the two ascended to the Christian Paradise.

Before releasing him from my power, I asked the archangel what would happen to His Lordship in the next world.

He assured me that the *Pan* and the *Pani* would be reunited and that their souls would live in eternal bliss together.

With the lord and lady of the castle dead and the demon banished, I decided to leave before questions were asked about my part in what had transpired. So my wife and I packed our belongings, paid a stable hand to drive us in an old coach, and made our way to her relatives in Lithuania. We said whatever we had to say to allay any suspicion, and I established myself in a new business.

I abandoned the study of hidden mysteries and dark powers. I spent my time instead studying simple moral texts that lifted my spirit without any pretensions to greater wisdom or power. I even let the gossips snicker that I was a bit of an ignoramus—let them think that, I told myself, if only they knew the awful price of too much learning about the universe's secrets.

And thus I lived on until Your Lordship's summons. So there you have it: the true tale of your grandparents.

Reb Nathan had spoken for so long that the moon had become exhausted and fallen to sleep beneath the horizon, and the pink cheerful light of the new dawn peeked through the window into the room.

He looked at the young Count, whose face was streaked with silently shed tears. The young *Pan* smiled through his sad, tired cheeks and thanked the old Jewish sorcerer for saving his grandfather's soul.

Reb Nathan thanked him for his kind words.

But I have one last question, the young Count continued, what happened to the monk, Brother Medardus? Why had he disappeared?

Nu, it is hard to say, Your Lordship. When I emerged from the dungeon he was nowhere to be found. Nor did any of the servants see him leave. He had vanished—poof!—into the air.

But I did hear something later. After I had been settled in Lithuania for a few years, a rumor reached us about a Christian monk named Brother Medardus who had died in Podolia. The monk had been found dead underneath the monastery in the underground crypts. Near the corpse were instruments of demonic rites—forbidden books listing the names of evil spirits, circles drawn on the ground with unusual symbols. They found a girl down there chained to a wall, a shivering, terrified creature—he had apparently done unspeakable things to her.

So perhaps Lady Ewa should not have put her trust in such a man. Maybe Brother Medardus had been seduced by Halinka, or maybe he had never ceased to be a servant of her sister demons, despite pretending to repent. Who knows these things? But I am sure that, in the next world, your grandparents are treated with great honor and enjoy every luxury, while the depraved monk is getting his just reward in *gehenna*.

The young Count nodded his agreement somewhat absently and did not press for further details. Nathan was not sure if the interview was concluded; exhausted as he was, he did not wish to offend His Lordship by leaving before he was permitted to do so.

The young *Pan* stood up, walked to the window, and suddenly smiled at the rising sun as if it had just given him the most wonderful news. He rubbed his chin and then turned back to Nathan.

I had been convinced that this house had been an abode of depravity. The pagan gardens, the rumors of black masses at night, your tales of my grandfather's affair with the demon maiden. But you have now revealed to me that, to the contrary, this castle is a place of great holiness and sanctity—this castle should be a shrine to the power of Our Savior to extend the grace of salvation to even the most wicked and corrupt soul.

As you are a Jew, I imagine you do not know the story of Theophilus?

Reb Nathan shook his head.

Theophilus was a priest who lived hundreds of years ago. After his rivals bested him in the scramble for worldly glory and honor, in his bitterness he summoned the devil and made a terrible pact: He renounced his faith in Christ Our Lord and the salvation of his soul in exchange for the power to vanquish and punish his enemies.

But Theophilus later realized the error of his ways, and repented and begged forgiveness from the Holy Virgin Mother. She overcame the snares and the nets of the Evil One and brought Theophilus back to the Christian fold, and through the grace of her love he was saved.

When you summoned a saint to save my grandfather, it must have been Theophilus—what other saint could truly understand what he had been through and his terrible grief and guilt? Yes, it must have been Theophilus who came. I will relay my grandfather's tale—with your name discreetly omitted—to the bishop, and we shall make this ruin into a shrine and a monument to Christ and His infinite wonders and mercies and glories. Christians far and wide need to know this story—that miraculous grace still descends upon us from Heaven, that we are not forsaken, but loved and cherished by Our Creator.

Nathan shrugged his shoulders. These matters are beyond me, he said. I do not know what it is like to walk in a bishop's dream.

VI. How the Sorcerer Was Truly Saved

A RESTLESSNESS HAD drawn Reb Nathan back into the ruins of the old castle gardens. The afternoon was sunny and still—not even the hint of a breeze, not even the slightest hum of a bird or an insect. After absentmindedly meandering through the overgrown paths, he came to an artificial grotto, inside of which was a blue-veined marble bench shaped like a horseshoe. When the old *Pan* had maintained these gardens in their original splendor, the floor and the bench would be doused with salt water and seaweed, as if the cave really were an isolated haunt by the seashore—perhaps, the old Count would muse, a spot where Odysseus would have washed up on his travels.

My dear Nathan, he once asked, do you know that Odysseus, the great hero, once landed on an island with a witch? But then he overcame her and made her his lover?

Nathan replied that he did not know about this man and his witch, but the infernal powers had been attacking and tormenting humanity ever since Creation. The old lord had laughed and walked away.

Reb Nathan sat down upon the bench. He put his hands on the smooth, hard marble, but then withdrew them quickly. His heart suddenly beat fast, and he realized why this grotto seemed so familiar—it was here, yes, on this bench, under the light of a wild yellow moon, that he had fornicated with Halinka.

It had been like no earthly act. With his wife, his Shayne, he would grow excited, blood flowed fast, his mind raced and floated away, then a fast release and it was done. The experience was akin to the onset of a sudden sickness, with the same feelings of exhaustion and desolation afterwards.

But with Halinka he had felt as if the sparks of holiness—the pieces of divinity scattered and trapped at Creation—were being lovingly excavated from within him, from a place so deeply buried in the dark recess of his soul that he had never perceived it clearly. As the sparks rose to his lips, Nathan felt that the physical barriers that separated him from the rest of Creation were dissolving and that he was now a part of all things, that everything was joined together as an aspect of the unknowable infinity and unity of the Holy One, Blessed be He, Whose presence and majesty filled the whole universe.

When Halinka finished the act, there was a falling away from that divine unity, as if he had been dancing to the most beautiful melody, but then had tripped and fallen over a cliff behind him, tumbling too far down to hear the music anymore. Overwhelmed by the sudden gain and loss of true bliss, Reb Nathan exploded in sobs.

Halinka took his hand. My poor learned scholar, did I not tell you that the holy sparks were real and that my embrace could reveal to you the wonders of the universe? Stay with me, love me, and we will raise each other's divine sparks trapped in this awful *kelipah*, this husk of gross physicality, and we shall ascend to His glorious throne together.

Reb Nathan had become Halinka's lover after the death of the old *Pan*. For he had lied to the young Count—he had not cast the demon away. Nor had he arranged for the old *Pan* to confess his sins and receive absolution.

Nathan had not been shackled in the dungeon, but rather the *Pani* had ordered him to his rooms with his wife and family. And there he had sat, trying to study a holy book while his Shayne, hysterical and screaming, rained curses upon his head. What was to become of them? Did her husband have a hand in the *Pan*'s disgusting adultery with the Turkish serving girl? How could the *Pani* not exact the most dreadful retribution? Could he at least try to see if Her Ladyship would have mercy on the children? But no baptism—if it came to that, if that was to be the ransom of their lives; better to die as martyrs for *Kiddush HaShem*. And on and on she had moaned and gesticulated.

Until finally there was a knock at the door. A young page in full livery announced that Reb Nathan had been ordered to re-enter the presence of Lady Ewa. Shayne fell suddenly silent and visibly trembled. Relieved at the opportunity to escape his wife's anxieties and accusations, Nathan quickly followed the page to Her Ladyship's bedroom.

The bedroom had been painted a cheerful sky blue in those bygone days, and the walls had been hung with paintings of shepherds in pretty green fields with their country brides. There were wide windows facing east, so that in the morning the room was flooded with sunlight.

But Nathan had been summoned in the dead of night, when the dull moonbeams cast only a faint glow. In the room, next to the bed, was a table with two burning candles. In between them was a golden platter on which rested the decapitated head of Lady Ewa.

He stumbled backward and let out a cry which he tried, and failed, to stifle. Then a laugh came from the bed. He turned towards the direction of the sound, and there was Halinka sprawled upon the sheets, wearing only an immodest red silk robe.

What is this? What awful crime have you committed?

Halinka sighed but betrayed no sign of fear. Rather, she slowly explained that Lady Ewa had made the most horrible accusations against her character and her moral conduct, including the outrageous claim that she was poisoning the Count. The *Pani* had sent a servant out on horseback to fetch the local priest, whom Halinka knew from her sisters to be a deeply intolerant, hateful man, a murderous fanatic bound to send her away or worse.

She had needed to act to prevent terrible, unjust punishments being inflicted upon her. He could see that, right? She did what had to be done. One of her dearest friends—a fellow demon—took the shape of a she-wolf and attacked the servant's horse at the bend of the road near the monastery. With the horse's legs broken, the servant could not reach the parish priest. But he naturally went instead to find a clergyman at the monastery and thus fulfill his mission.

This was exactly how Halinka had planned to defend herself. For one of the monks in the abbey, Brother Medardus, had long been the lover of Halinka's sister. This Brother Medardus had been raised as an orphan in a monastery in Germany, where he had been a deeply pious boy. As a young man he became famous for his fervent sermons denouncing sin and demanding penitence, sermons so powerful that great lords fell to their knees and, tears flooding their cheeks, begged the chapel's statue of the Virgin Mary to forgive them for all their wicked deeds.

Lauded, almost worshipped, at such a tender age, Brother Medardus grew vain. He was thus easily seduced by a demon in the guise of a beautiful young noblewoman, who had asked that he be her confessor. She would recount garish scenes of wild carnal excess to him—ostensibly to unburden her heart with a full and forthright confession. One day she invited him to her rooms late at night. She said she wanted to thank him for all his kindness and attention—he was such a good and pious man, and she was so awful, she had done such disgusting, shameful things. She served him a cup of wine—a very special wine, which clouded his reason and roused his bodily lusts. He broke his monastic vows with the demon lady that night doing wicked, immoral acts.

He had enjoyed these repulsive deeds so greatly that he could not bring himself to stop and repent. After gossip spread about the affair, he left for an abbey in Podolia, far from prying eyes—a crumbling establishment in the thick woods that had been built long ago by missionaries to the once savage pagan Slavs. He would descend deep into the monastery's underground catacombs at night, where his demon mistress would come to him.

But there was a price for her favors. He had to perform small errands for her and her kind—defacing sacred books or relics so they lost their holy power, or helping to lead a poor soul into temptation.

As Halinka had arranged with her demon sister, this Brother Medardus volunteered to return to the castle with the *Pani*'s servant. Upon arrival he had first gone to see the old *Pan*, whom he promptly diagnosed as the victim of witchcraft and sorcery. Lady Ewa seethed—she swore she had known it all along, and she was certain that Halinka was to blame. She planned to torture Halinka until her husband was cured and then to burn the witch to ashes.

Brother Medardus followed the *Pani* to Halinka's room. There Her Ladyship hurled the most awful accusations—witch, whore, murderer. Halinka begged her to reconsider these cruel words, explaining meekly to Lady Ewa that her husband had forced her to satisfy his most debased lusts against her will. It was he who had demanded that she heighten his pleasure with dark sorcery, even though she had warned him of the dangers. The *Pan* had threatened to kill her if she dared to refuse him. Could not the Countess, in her mercy and goodness, see that Halinka was innocent of any crime?

Lady Ewa spat on the ground in response and ordered Brother Medardus to recite an incantation to exorcise the evil powers that had brought such corruption into the castle. The monk began intoning words quickly in Latin. The room went completely dark. When the candles showed their light again,

Her Ladyship's headless body lay on the floor while her severed head sat on a gold platter.

The monk dutifully placed the body in the hearth, lit the fire, and burned the remains of the *Pani* below the neck. He then bowed, took his leave, and departed in a black carriage waiting for him at the gate.

So, dear Reb Nathan, that is how the *Pani*'s head ended up here in the state it is in. But you understand, don't you, that I had no other choice? She wanted to do me harm, even though I had not wronged her. I did not seek this place out—you summoned me here, and you made me appear in this form. Then he insisted upon taking his pleasure with me, again and again. I told him I was not like a human woman, that there could be consequences. But he ignored me and indulged his appetites every chance he had.

Nathan had been unsettled by Halinka's tale, but then he had thought: She is a demon—what did you expect? He had warned the *Pan* that summoning her was a foolish idea.

Where is the *Pan* now? he asked her.

Where everyone left him—in his bed.

Halinka smiled slightly, stepped over to Nathan, and grabbed him by the hands. She stared up intensely into his eyes until he felt his limbs tremble and the sweat from his body drip into his clothes. Then she turned to the door and led Nathan by the hand, like an obedient small boy, through the winding halls to the old Count's bed.

The old *Pan* groaned miserably when they approached him. There seemed to be almost no life remaining under his wrinkled blue-grey skin. Halinka released her grip, and Nathan approached his friend's bedside.

In a gasping, hollow voice, the *Pan* asked if it was him, Nathan?

Yes, My Lord, it is me.

Save me, he said. You must save me. That monster, that whore, murdered my Ewa, my love, the mother of my sons. Cast her back—do it, now, send her away, and summon a priest to hear my confession … I heard the scream … Ewa's terrible scream, when it happened. Then the servants told me. We must—

But his strength then failed him, and he fell backwards into a cavernous pillow. His breath rose and fell slowly in agonized wheezes and his eyelids half-covered his beseeching eyes; saliva dribbled from his mouth and down his chin and throat.

Nathan turned his gaze back to Halinka. He knew he should cast her back—she was a demon, and the murder of the *Pani* and the depleting of the soul of the *Pan* would no doubt be just the start of her many crimes. Yet he felt such stabbing pains in his flesh at the thought of not being in her presence.

Halinka approached him again and took his hand into hers.

Please do not do cast me away, good Reb Nathan. You know there is a spark of holiness inside me. Is it not true that, without a spark of the Holy One's radiance scattered at Creation, I could not live? There are dark forces that pull me towards evil things. And this vile, disgusting lecher and fornicator has only made it worse—he forced you to conjure me here, against my will and yours, to be a plaything, a toy doll, for his shameful, gross bodily lusts. How can I be called depraved when you and men like you use all your might to fling me down into the filth?

But you can stop this, you can save me. You know how the Messiah, Sabbatai Zevi, apostatized from holy Israel in order to delve deeply into the evil of the *kelipah* of the Gentile world and thus redeem the holy sparks trapped there. My divine spark of light, which is pleading with you now, is also trapped in the *kelipah*, where you and he have wedged it in more deeply. Don't you see how you have undermined the Messianic mission by driving me into greater darkness and sin?

With your great learning and scholarship, I know you can help me. Love me, teach me, be my companion and guide. Please, I beg you, help me. It is not me who merits casting back to the burning tar pits of *gehenna*—it is him, with his revolting appetites and ever greater demands for filthier, more loathsome orgies. Cast him back.

Nathan reflected; she was right: Nothing can live without a divine spark, and so all the creatures of darkness—including this demon—needed such a spark from which to draw their strength. Maybe that spark, sensing the presence of a learned Jew, was trying to escape from its prison in the demonic husk. If Our Lord the Messiah Sabbatai Zevi himself had seen the need to excavate the holy sparks imprisoned deep within the belly of the infernal realms, could Nathan not raise this one spark quivering before him?

And he had driven her deep into sin with the old Count—he alone was responsible, he had misused his learning for wicked ends. He should have resisted the *Pan*'s threats. What would it matter if he had been cut down and thus lost this world of illusion and lies? His soul would have ascended to a higher sphere.

But then he reflected further: This terrible abuse of the holiness within Halinka was not his fault—he had acted under duress. He was not responsible. He had never attempted such a conjuring until forced by the gravest threats, not to himself, but to his children—yes, his children, he had no choice but to do what he had to do to keep them safe. Halinka was right—there was only one criminal, and it was the *Pan*. And now he wanted to compound his crimes by sending her away like a spoiled child discarding his worn out doll.

Nathan felt rage swell within him. The *Pan*, he thought, is the true demon—he is the corrupter. If I help him again now, I will only aid his crimes in the future.

Halinka squeezed his hand tightly. She then moved that hand and placed it over the old Count's mouth and nose. Feeling compelled by an uncontrollable rage and disgust, Nathan continued to press his hand with all his strength until the *Pan* ceased his labored breathing, and what was left of his soul departed from his wasted, dead body.

It took Nathan a moment to grasp the awful crime he had committed, but then he fell to his knees and sobbed. Halinka kneeled down next to him and assured him that the old Count had been on the verge of death regardless—his passage had just been eased, the deed was an act of mercy, a kindness. And there was no use moaning over the dead—he could not undo what had been done. But she still was there and she needed his help.

So he agreed to help Halinka.

When he returned to his rooms, Nathan told Shayne of the death of the *Pan*, although he carefully concealed his own hand in events. His wife insisted they leave immediately—this place was cursed, she said, and we should not linger here waiting until that demon witch devours us, too.

But then Nathan calmly explained that they were to stay, at least a little longer. While Halinka had been in the grip of dark forces, she still possessed—like all living things—a spark of light within her that had once emanated from the Holy One, Blessed be He. Nathan could not abandon her to the infernal realms without first trying to raise that spark of holiness.

Shayne burst with rage at these words: You idiot! She is a foul beast and a murderer. She has seduced you, hasn't she? Your lusts are as disgusting as the Count's. Get away from me.

And she grabbed her husband and pushed him out the door.

Reb Nathan remembered how he had stood in that hallway brimming with indignation. How could she make such terrible accusations against him? He who had done so much to provide for her and the children. He was tempted to meet her evil words with even more evil words of his own. But he stopped his tongue; he would not cause more anguish and upheaval in his household. Let her calm herself down.

And so instead of raining curses upon her head, Reb Nathan quietly walked away from his wife's bed. It was still night and quite dark, but in his restlessness he entered the gardens. He had wandered to the artificial grotto where he now sat remembering these events. Back then it was filled with the scents of the sea—salt water and seaweed. And there had been a statue there—a small one, yes—a small man with an angry face and a big trident.

Halinka joined him on the bench inside the grotto and asked why he was so troubled. He recounted his quarrel with Shayne, but was adamant that he would not listen to his wife's slanders against her because he knew there was a divine spark in her to be raised.

You are a good man, a righteous man, she reassured him. You can see beneath these surface illusions of good and evil, of human and demon. You can see the hidden truth—others cannot, but you, you with your great learning, can see the spark of light trapped inside me. You have saved me—first from that horrible Count, who dragged me into the deepest abyss of sin, now from your cruel, heartless wife.

Moving close to him, she pulled his head down towards her mouth, but did not kiss him. Look down my throat, she said, look down inside me—you can see it, you can smell it. Reb Nathan moved his eyes to the space between those red lips and peered down. There was a faint glow from within and a smell of honey and flowers. The glow and the fragrance excited him, and he found himself drawn toward them. Soon he was kissing her lips; soon their bodies were entwined and naked. When it was over Nathan was certain he had seen a vision of true holiness and pure light that he longed to experience again.

As he and Halinka did not part until dawn, he slept all the next day and awoke at dusk. He had no desire to be in the company of his wife, with her ignorant rage and petty reproaches; he yearned only to return to that ecstatic delight he had found in Halinka's arms.

After sunset, Nathan strolled in the moonlit gardens with Halinka. Gilded carriages arrived at the castle gate, whose passengers joined them. There were two other demon women, both appearing in the guise of beautiful human maidens, and there were several demon men who appeared in the costume of learned Jewish sages. All night he alternated between studying with the men—who had thoughtfully brought lamps that provided enough light to read their esoteric manuscripts filled with obscure wisdom—and fornicating with the demon women, all of whom were able to raise him to fantastic visions of holiness as Halinka had done. Between the texts he studied and the rapturous bliss he experienced, Nathan believed he had begun to see far more deeply into the true structure of the universe that lay beyond the base, deceptive physical world in which his soul was trapped during this life.

When the sun rose these companions departed and Halinka laid him to bed, where he collapsed into a deep, dreamless sleep. He felt like a stiff animal corpse lying inert in a ditch.

Nathan lost track of time as he lived only in and for these enchanted garden nights. Days certainly passed, maybe weeks. He did not think it had been months, but he could not be sure—it was difficult to remember. What he recalled clearly were the sensations he had felt: excitement and exaltation and desire, followed by an exhaustion so deep as to be unnatural and inhuman. He thought nothing of his wife and children, or the dead Count and Countess, or anything else but his wondrous nocturnal revels.

He also did not notice how weak he had become. Shayne later told him how alarmed she had been as his weight seemed to melt away and wrinkles began to crop up in his pale skin. But at night, in the grottoes and in the temples of love and in the winding paths, he always felt young and strong. Halinka and her sisters would marvel at how handsome and virile he was, how they found his lovemaking to be so tiring for their feebler frames.

But then the beautiful idyll was shattered. Nathan recalled he had been in a grotto—yes, he was sure, the same one where he sat now after all these years—fornicating with Halinka and her sisters. His soul had vaulted to the highest heights of Paradise, where he could see the Messiah, Sabbatai Zevi, dance with ecstasy around the Tree of Life. Sabbatai reached out his hand to Nathan and urged him to pluck the wondrous fruit—so large and pink and ripe—and satisfy his thirst and hunger. Taste the fruits of the Garden of Eden, Sabbatai had said, and new worlds will open to your eyes.

Yet before Nathan could pick the fruit, the vision suddenly disappeared. He again saw only the grotto, which now looked absurd to him—a painfully fake seaside cave that was nowhere near the actual sea.

There were shouts and screams, but he could not make out what was being said. When he turned his head toward Halinka and her sisters, he no longer beheld alluring, voluptuous women. Instead he now saw scaly, hissing creatures with writhing snakes for hair and hooves for feet. There were insects crawling everywhere, large black buzzing beetles.

He stood up and tried to leave but, dizzy and weak, he staggered about until he fell down in a corner. He saw, for the first time, that his skin was wasting away, waxen and wrinkled. The black buzzing beetles crawled up his legs and arms, but he was too feeble to fight them off. Their little mouths gnawed eagerly at his flesh. He was sure this was his end. It was clear to him now that he had sinned terribly—he had murdered the old *Pan* with his own hands—and he must accordingly suffer the fitting punishment. Tears of shame and pain flowed swiftly down his cheeks.

And yet, in another instant, the beetles had vanished, as had the demons. Nathan was panting on the ground, still unable to believe that the pests were gone. Then a hand reached out and helped him to stand again. Looking up he saw his wife, Shayne, calm and smiling, who led him slowly—for his arthritic limbs found walking to be hard—back to the bench.

In her hand was a wooden flask. By the moonlight, Nathan could see the many Hebrew letters carved on its surface which formed countless variations of the most potent secret names for the Holy One, Blessed be He. She gently leaned his head back, opened his mouth, and poured water from the flask down his throat.

Nathan had never tasted anything so sweet. The liquid flowed rapidly through his veins, and everywhere it went, he felt himself healed. The wrinkles faded away, his color returned, his muscles swelled and bulged, and the stiffness in his joints withered away.

Shayne now explained how she had cast away the demons and saved her husband. After the deaths of the *Pan* and the *Pani*, she had been desperate to flee this awful castle. But her Nathan had fallen under the spell of the demon witch, tricked by her cunning words and her illusions of physical beauty. She had tried to speak to him, tried to get him to acknowledge his frightened, shivering children, but his eyes could not see. He had looked upon his wife and children as if they were so many broken chairs strewn about the cellar floor.

She asked the servants for help, but they only cursed her in response: Dirty Jew, you brought this evil into our home and killed our master and mistress. Get away!

So she fasted and prayed. She begged the Holy One, Blessed be He, to send aid to her. And in His Infinite Mercy and Abundant Goodness, He did so. A beggar showed up at the castle gates asking for alms. Because he was a Jew, the servants sent him to Shayne. She fed him, and helped him to wash, and mended some of his garments. He played with the children and told them tales of the holy sages who had lived long ago, may their memory be for a blessing.

The beggar praised her as a good and virtuous woman. But where, he asked, is your husband? A man with a wife as noble as you must himself be a fine man, too, and maybe even a scholar who could share a few words of Torah with me. Now that my belly has eaten its full, my soul seeks to satisfy its hunger with the sustenance of the Torah.

Shayne looked down, ashamed and unable to answer.

Are you a widow?

She shook her head no.

Then where has your husband gone?

And now Shayne burst into tears and collapsed into a tiny ball on the floor. She could not bear the shame of her husband's sinful behavior.

The beggar reached down and lifted her up from the floor. When her eyes beheld him again, his face was radiant and smiling kindly. I can help you, he assured her. Because you have shown such kindness to a beggar and performed the *mitzvah* of hospitality with such zeal and devotion—like your Father Abraham, may he rest in peace—you have merited two gifts that can save your husband from the spells of Lilith's demon daughters. This amulet will drive away the demons' powers of illusion and cast them back to their realm. Simply hold it up before them and recite aloud the words that will appear to be floating in the air before your eyes. This flask contains water from the streams that flow in the Garden of Eden. Give it to your husband to drink, and it will heal the wounds in his body and soul.

Shayne looked closely at the two objects the beggar had given her, the exquisitely carved wooden flask and the green jade amulet. When she looked up again to ask him how he knew about the demons—for, out of shame, she had said nothing about them—he had disappeared. And then she knew that the Holy One, Blessed be He, had sent His Prophet Elijah to her aid. She gripped the two gifts tightly and offered a heartfelt prayer of thanks.

After nightfall she had walked confidently into the gardens, where she found her husband in this grotto doing filthy, unspeakably disgusting acts with three demon women. She grasped the amulet and raised it high above her head. Suddenly, in the air, written in clear Yiddish, she saw an incantation which she rapidly recited. The demons shrieked, their masks fell off, and they dissolved into the air. And then her husband was healed by the waters of the Garden of Eden.

Nathan fell at his wife's feet, thanked her for saving him, and begged her forgiveness.

I forgive you, she said calmly. Because you were under the spell of a demon witch, you did not have control of your reason. It is not that you consciously chose to sin with another woman. But I also know that you alone of this household had the esoteric wisdom to conjure that demon. I will not shame you and accuse you publicly—I know you were acting under compulsion, that this was not truly your desire, and I will not imperil our children's ability to strike fine marriage matches by staining your name. However, my forgiveness has a price: We leave this place tomorrow at dawn. We will travel to my relatives in Lithuania, far from here, where you will start a new business. You will not summon demons again or delve into mysteries that should stay hidden. You will be a righteous and upstanding Jew, you will study the Psalms and not the *Kabbalah*, you will inspire confidence in good Jewish householders so that they can marry their children to ours.

Nathan mutely obeyed. While at first the shock of events had struck him speechless, later it was prudence that made him hold his tongue: because even though he knew that his conduct had been wicked and shameful, he still longed for Halinka. While his wife agreed to lay with him again, the pleasures she offered were so meager compared to the exhilaration of embracing the demon. It is as if, he thought, I have traded the sweetest, most luxurious Tokay wine for the brine of pickled cucumbers.

He never spoke of Halinka or his adventure with the *Pan*, until the *Pan*'s grandson had summoned him to return here. He had followed Shayne's instructions, which he knew to be proper and just. His business thrived in Lithuania, and he was much honored for his piety and devotion to learning (and he was also quite careful to conceal his faith in the Lord Messiah Sabbatai Zevi, even from the Messiah's other secret adherents). His children made fine matches. His wife was a supremely happy woman; she practically skipped through the marketplace and the women's section of the synagogue, so thankful was she for the blessings bestowed upon her by the Holy One, Blessed be He. She gave generously to charity and provided instruction in the laws of purity to young brides.

But through all these years, Nathan had been haunted by his secret sadness and longing. While he enjoyed the blessings of this world, these still paled in comparison to the delights and visions he had once experienced in Halinka's embrace. In his new life as a pious householder, he felt as if he was playacting in a world that was not quite real. He had seen the hidden, inner world of truth in the demon's arms, but now he was assaulted with dull chatter about petty concerns—about marriage matches and buying clothes and repairing rotting beams in the synagogue. How could he care for such puny things when he had once scaled such lofty heights?

Nathan had sometimes pondered summoning Halinka back to him. But he recalled the *Pan*'s fate, and thought of his wife and children, and put such desires aside, no matter how hotly they burned in him. Yet he felt wronged by this sacrifice. There were moments when he saw Shayne directing the servants or advising her daughter-in-law, a serene and kind matron grown robustly plump, with her plain face stretched and puffed out from many too delicacies, and he was filled with hatred. Why had he denied himself visions of great knowledge and even greater pleasures just to appease this stupid cow?

Yet such moments of bitterness would pass away. He would then feel ashamed of having judged his wife so harshly, and feel even more ashamed at his inability to let go of his disgusting youthful lusts.

Shayne had died peacefully. One night she had gone to sleep and the Angel of Death had gently harvested her soul. The matchmakers, as was their wont when a rich husband became a rich widower, peddled many matches to him, but he was not interested. Shayne's death had left him empty and lonely, but he could not betray her again by lying in the arms of another woman.

Nathan did not understand how he could still be living on without her. It had been the Holy One's will to save him for the sake of her prayers and righteous deeds. So why was he allotted such a long life, while she had been taken away from her children and grandchildren, whom she had loved so dearly?

In his reverie, he had sat so long in the grotto that it was now twilight. With difficulty, his legs hoisted his body upright once more, and he walked slowly in the pink light back to the castle.

Tears rolled thickly down his cheeks. He knew now, in the marrow of his bones, that his life had been a bitter failure.

Other Books by Barak Bassman

Elegy of the Minotaur

Repentance: A Tale of Demons in Old Jewish Poland

King Solomon and Ashmedai: A Wisdom Tale

The Twilight of the Magical Siren: A Tale of Late Antiquity

The Leper Princess and The Court Jew

The Last Confession of Joseph della Reina

The Gifts of the Fairy Melusine